céili

MORIAH GEMEL

interlude press • new york

interlude ❤ press • new york

To Mom: Thank you for letting me read books way beyond my reading level, especially the ones that contained naughty bits.

1

THE ONLY THING DEVON NOTICES as he tosses back his third shot is that the bar smells like old peanut butter. Bars shouldn't smell like that. It's not dignified. They should smell like beer and remorse, or fruity cocktails and sweat, or olives and piano music.

Does piano music have a smell?

"Hey," Devon says, nodding at the bartender. The man turns and cocks an ear. "Does piano music have a smell?"

The bartender's face is impressive in its instant shift to suspicion. "How many have you had tonight?"

"Three."

"I mean overall."

"Three."

"Lightweight?"

As someone whose family is Irish all the way back on both sides, despite his dark skin, Devon takes offense. "No. It's a legitimate question."

"You're asking if music smells."

"I meant like does a piano have a smell? Like, piano oil. I've never played piano."

"I think we're gonna cut you off," the bartender says. "Pay your tab and call a cab, okay?"

"Hey—"

But the bartender is across the bar already, tending to a patron who probably doesn't ask silly questions. So Devon sighs, pulls out his wallet and slaps a twenty on the bar before he heads for the door.

There has to be another bar nearby where he can drown his sorrows, right? He's not familiar with this part of town. He's only here because he had a meeting with a potential agent. However, it's another letdown later, and he's still not in the mood to go home. He wants to wallow. But apparently he can't wallow out loud, or he gets cut off after only three shots.

A cab is out of the question. Maybe he'll catch the next bus, or maybe even walk; it's not *that* far from Sunset to Echo Park. But he has no desire to go back to his tiny, empty apartment that will no doubt be filled with the sounds of his upstairs neighbor stomping around to the tune of some nameless band that has less talent than Devon but a record deal anyway, fuck it all.

Fucking hipsters. Devon would probably be considered one himself, but fuck them anyway.

Devon steps outside and breathes for a minute. It smells like L.A.: grease and heat and asphalt and tourists and something else he usually doesn't smell—maybe something Sunset-y? Something sharp and alive and brisk, something unique to this part of town, something—

Drip. Drip. Devon tilts his face up, and water patters on his face and hands. Of all nights, of all times, Los Angeles has decided to *rain.*

Devon has a choice. Left is the way home, to darkness and solitude. Few friends, distant family, two jobs that pay the bills but provide no satisfaction, no luck, no plan for the future that has any chance of success, just dreams, wispy and wretched. He has a bed with a dip in the middle, thin sheets, a threadbare carpet. He has a leaky faucet and creaky floorboards. He has not a whole lot else.

Right is the unknown. It's wandering, freedom; it's a long, drenched night but enough time and space to think without the cloying weight of familiarity. It's the sidewalk and the streets and building after building after building and no destination in mind. It's potentially, likely nothing, but possibly everything.

Devon turns right.

AIMLESS IS PROBABLY THE BEST way to describe two things in Devon's life: the way he walks the city in the rain that night, and pretty much the rest of his life altogether. He grew up a single child to boring, average parents in a small town a few hours out of Boston. At school he was the only child in his class with dark skin; the only child in his class with immigrant parents, too. His accent got him teased, and by the time he graduated there was not a lilt in his words to be found. To be tolerated, though never well-liked or loved—that was his life. Unable to handle his unhappiness themselves, his parents had him go to a couple different therapists a few times; he quit as a teenager but kept a doctor of record to prescribe the pills that to this day keep him from too much darkness. But otherwise he drifted through, and then drifted through college, and then drifted to L.A. to make it as a singer-songwriter, he and his guitar (and his savings account, which dwindles after two unsuccessful years, no matter how much he works).

It fits, then, that he takes every turn he comes across, left and right mattering little. The sidewalks are mostly even, so Devon's body shifts into automatic; his thoughts take over while his body wanders past building after building with no distinction until he's thoroughly lost. And isn't that just apropos? He's been lost all his life, because he never had anyone to guide him. His parents didn't bother; they were too busy working. He never had any close friends. He was too distant, too strange, too angry from the very start, with only his need for *something*, for some kind of love, driving him. It's never helped that he's had mental illnesses on the clock since he was small. He started his life melancholy, and it grew into depression. And it seemed no one could understand.

His shirt sticks to his back. How uncomfortable. But that's not a feeling he's not used to. He's faced plenty of discomfort in his life: discomfort with his parents, the distance between him and them; discomfort with kids in his school, who would rather mock than sympathize; discomfort with his therapists, who attributed him with diagnosis after diagnosis that never seemed to fit or explain anything.

So he drifted. He made it through one day at a time, and that turned into weeks and months and years. And he still hasn't found something to ground him.

But now he is well and truly lost, in the literal sense. He knows he headed west, but with however many turns he's taken, he could be facing any direction, and the cloudy, city-lit night sky won't help him pretend he can navigate by the stars.

So he walks. He walks until his feet ache and a blister forms on his right heel. He walks until he's soaked in the light rain, until he can't walk anymore. He walks until he really does have to go home. It's not late, but he's walked for hours, and he's exhausted and he has to pee.

He has no idea where he is. But a building ahead has a bright neon sign, and maybe someone inside can point him in the right direction. It takes up its little block all by itself, dark but for the bright neon sign. Devon walks up and squints at it.

Céilí. Blue, cursive script. That's all it says—no *open* sign, no drink signs, no windows on the first floor at all; they start on the second floor and reach up to the top, maybe three more stories up. Just *Céilí* over the heavy double doors.

It could be a private club. Maybe a strip joint, trying to be discreet. The meaning of the name niggles at Devon, as if he heard it somewhere, but can't place it.

Devon shrugs to himself and pulls open the door. Nothing spectacular at first glance—there's a short, dark hallway to another pair of double doors, but these have windows in them and there's light beyond, warm and welcoming. He can hear music and chatter—thank god, someone's there. He walks forward and pulls open a second door and lets himself inside.

On stage, two girls and a guy in tight, skimpy clothing twirl and gyrate together. It's a burlesque number, meant to be appealing and sensuous. They all slink, all feminine, even the guy, and Devon nods to himself. *That's cool. This place might be welcoming to people like him.*

But then, in a single surreal moment, all chatter dims, and every head in the place turns to Devon though the performance goes on on stage. In the main part of the room, several round wooden tables are occupied to greater or lesser extents, so the room is about half full. And every single eye is turned to Devon. He freezes, and his eyes dart to and from each pair of the eyes that are focused on him.

Oh no. Did he walk into a private club? Is this place by invitation only? Is it the mafia? The dead air hangs too heavy, and Devon doesn't feel comfortable

with this many stares, even if he is a performer. Usually the stares feel less—
focused. It's a sea of facelessness beyond bright lights, not—all these faces,
right there, directed right at him. He feels *seen*, well and truly seen as he has
never felt in all his life. Cold buzzing tingles its way up his spine; it brings up
goose bumps on his arms, and he licks his dry lips nervously. *Shit*.

Across the room, a bartender nods at him and then beckons. He doesn't
look unfriendly or threatening. He just crooks one hand, waving Devon
forward. He's offering a save to Devon, maybe, or he very well might throw
him out. But it's an invitation, one Devon takes gratefully. He strides over
as though he belongs, ignoring the chatter that picks up as he walks. At least
it's better than the silence.

"New here?" the bartender asks. He has blue hair and a piercing in his lip.
Otherwise, he's average; there's nothing spectacular about his face: ordinary
brown eyes, no noticeable cheekbones, thin lips, straight nose.

"Yes," Devon says. "First time. What is this place?"

The bartender blinks at him as though he can't believe his eyes. "Huh.
Really?"

Devon shakes his head, confused. "Um. Really."

"I'm Brandon," the bartender says, as he offers his hand. "Welcome to
Céilí."

Devon takes the hand and shakes it. "Devon Caelin."

Brandon's eyebrows raise. "Irish name?"

"Yes," Devon says. What does it matter? "Both sides."

"No kidding," Brandon says. He eyes Devon's half-Black skin, no doubt.
Devon sighs. All his life he was the object of curiosity, all through both high
school and college. Anyone who found out his name and knew its origins
couldn't square that with his color. *Narrow-minded, goddamn—*

"It happens." Devon glances up at the drinks menu and then pauses and
does a double take. *What the fuck.* "Um."

Aisling. Immrama Draught. What the hell kinds of drink names are those?

"What," Devon says uncertainly. He clears his throat; he should probably
not look like a dumbass right now. He wants to seem as though he belongs
here; he has to go along with it, right? Fit in so he doesn't look like a complete
fool. He might as well order a drink. "I'll have a—uh—*nenadmim*."

The bartender's lips pull in and widen, and his eyes sparkle—but he doesn't laugh. He reaches under the bar and pulls out a large wooden ball with a spout on top; a strange, spherical wooden flask. Devon doesn't try to hide his confusion as Brandon pops a cork and pours the drink, a brown concoction.

"Here you go," Brandon says. He smiles and slides it over. Devon nods, takes the drink and sips politely. He hopes it's not poisoned, or weird homemade booze that was made in a garbage can, or—

It's cider. It's hard cider, tart and crisp. It tastes really good, actually.

"So is this a theme bar?" Devon asks carefully.

"You could say that," Brandon says. "Any guesses what theme? You said you're Irish."

"It's Celtic, right?" Devon guesses. The names sound vaguely Celtic, from what he knows, which admittedly isn't much. "But, the performance seems kind of regionless…"

The dancers are finished, now. They had been dressed in simple black outfits that lacked coverage in varying degrees. Devon scans the room. The other people aren't dressed up; they aren't playing at anything. The bar itself is all dark woods and low lighting, like any pub Devon's been to. But it has no pool tables or bar tables—all the tables are large wooden things, seating at least twelve each, and most of the patrons face the stage, which is to the left of the bar. Across from the stage, there's a closed curtain. Nothing else is remarkable—not a bit of it stands out.

"Well, sort of," Brandon says. "We welcome people of all backgrounds. But our patron is from the Celtic region. So the drinks are based on stuff he knows. But the performances are indeed regionless, as you said."

"So. No real theme, then?" Devon says, to keep the conversation going. He's still uncomfortable, after the weird reaction to his entrance and the weird drinks, and probably because he's still pretty soggy. "I mean, what does the name mean? Um—*kay-lee*?"

"Close. You have no idea, do you?" Brandon asks. He shakes his head as if Devon is missing something big. He considers leaving, but Brandon continues, "Let me get you a towel, okay? Then we'll talk."

"Oh," Devon says. He *is* still pretty damp, and it's a kind offer. "Thanks, yeah, a towel would be nice."

Brandon heads to a set of doors behind the bar, and Devon takes another sip of his drink as he glances around. It's very, very good, not like the swill he usually drinks: whatever's on sale at the liquor store or local dive bar. It's apple-y and woodsy and Devon really, really hopes he can afford it, that this isn't a ridiculous, trendy twenty-bucks-a-drink place. Knowing his luck, it probably is. He sips delicately so as not to waste a really good drink, thinking his way into his wallet to make sure he has at least enough for this one.

The stage remains empty while Devon waits, and his eyes scan from the tables to the main door opposite the bar, and he finds himself turning in his seat to stare at the curtain on the wall across from the stage. It's a thick embroidered thing, deep chocolate brown that's almost black, with gold thread in classic Celtic patterns, knots and vines and triangular points; it drapes across the wall as if there might be another stage behind it. *What kind of bar has a wall hanging that close to the tables, though? They must have a helluva bouncer, to keep rowdy customers from tearing it down or soaking it with flying drinks in case of a fight. Very pretty, but very mysterious.*

As are the people in the room, who have begun to stare at him again. They're average looking people, people you'd see any day on the street— men and women of various ages and genders and races and statures and even social classes. They're not remarkably pretty, or obviously rich, or dressed strangely. And their stares vary, too; some glance at him out of the corners of their eyes, some look at him casually, but one table near the front is completely focused on him, as though he might do something any minute and they don't want to miss it. Devon shifts uncomfortably and takes another sip of his drink. Suddenly, he very much wants to leave. He could easily slip out and try to find his way to someplace else, like a main road, where he can get his bearings. He's had a moment's rest; it shouldn't be a big deal. But he could wander in circles and not know what he's doing, and he should get directions before he leaves and ends up somewhere weirder.

Brandon returns with a full-sized white towel.

"Here," he says, proffering it. "Dry off."

He nods to someone, calling, "Kelsi!" Devon peeks to the side while toweling his head. Someone at the front table stands up: a Black girl with long, platinum-grey dreads and a tattoo around her neck. She steps up to the bar and begins tending to the few customers seated there and chatting amiably. *So the staff is obviously of a certain type, with the weird hair and the body mods.* Devon can dig that, at least.

When he turns back, Brandon isn't behind the bar. He's coming to sit next to Devon at one of the leather-cushioned bar stools. He's a tall guy, skinny but ropey, not lanky. He is in control of himself as he folds his long, skinnies-clad legs.

"So. Want another drink?" Brandon asks. "Kelsi will get it for you."

"No, thanks," Devon says. "I think I'm good." He pushes his mostly empty cup away and smiles back at Brandon. "Thanks for the towel."

"No problem," Brandon says. "But, hey, we should talk."

We should talk? What the hell kind of conversation starter is that, with a total stranger?

"About what?" Devon asks suspiciously.

"I just want to ask you a few questions," Brandon says. "Like where are you from?"

"Here," Devon answers instantly. *Why could this man possibly want to know? Does he seem like a bumpkin?* "L.A. Um. Originally Massachusetts."

"Adopted?"

Devon frowns. *What a strange assumption to make.* "No?"

"Ah. Um. Close with your parents?"

"Sort of," Devon hedges. Truth be told, he and his parents exchange one phone call every other week at most, and it's always awkward. They didn't know how to deal with a son who was melancholy all the time, who ran off across the country, and Devon's never really fit in with their white-picket-fence American Dream. But they've never abused him or anything, and Devon loves them, and they raised him. But telling a stranger all that would be as weird as the stranger asking if he was close to his parents. "Why do you ask?"

"Uh. I don't exactly know how to tell you."

The feeling of suspicion increases, and Devon pulls out his wallet. He doesn't have to put up with this stuff, he just has to get directions. "Look, I'll pay for my drink and ask you where the nearest bus stop is?"

"No, wait," Brandon says. "Look. Drink is on the house, okay? And—and I really have something to tell you before you leave, but you won't believe me if I come out and say it, okay?"

Suspicion still reigns, but Devon's curiosity is piqued. *What wouldn't I believe?* "Okay. So… how are we going to get through this conversation, then?"

"Look, just hear me out, okay?" Brandon says. Devon sighs, shrugs and throws up a hand, and Brandon nods excitedly. "Um. Okay, I have an idea. Let's get you another drink. Still on the house."

"Okay." His shots from earlier are well worn off, and one more of the ciders won't hurt him. "More of the same, then."

"Hey, Kelsi!" Brandon calls out. She comes over, a tall, imposing figure, with prominent muscles on her arms. She could be a boxer or an MMA fighter. "Another cider for our friend here."

She pours more into Devon's glass and pushes it across with a sly little smile. "Don't go overboard, honey."

"Hush," Brandon says. He turns back to Devon. "Ignore her. Just drink up, okay?"

"Okay," Devon says. He takes a few sips. It's really, really good. "Okay. So. What now? What did you want to tell me?"

"Just talking for now," Brandon says. "How did you get here?"

Devon sighs again, and settles himself in for a weird conversation to end a really weird night. "I walked."

"I mean how did you find this place?" Brandon clarifies. "Did you hear about it from someone?"

"No, I just walked up," Devon says. Brandon motions to urge him on, and he adds, "I was on Sunset, and I didn't feel like going home. So I walked around, kinda aimless. I got tired, and then when I looked up, this place was in front of me. So I thought I'd come in and ask for directions."

"Okay, that rules that out," Brandon says inexplicably. "Um. Next step then. I want you to think of a number. Any number."

Devon eyes him. "Seriously?"

"Yes! Any number at all. Make it hard."

"This is ridiculous," Devon says, but unbidden he thinks of a number. Reflex from somewhere; whenever anyone says what to think or not to think, a person thinks it.

"Three thousand and two."

Devon, who had thought *three thousand and two* a split second earlier, stares. "Seriously? What—"

"Let's do something harder. Take a sip."

Devon doesn't sip. He sets the drink down and pushes it away. His gut churns with sudden fear and anger at himself. *Fuck, why did I take a drink from a stranger?* "What's in the drink? Am I saying stuff out loud?"

"No! It's not a trick," Brandon says. "Look, I can explain once you believe in me, okay? Just go with it. Can you think of the name of your first girlfriend? Or boyfriend. Or whatever. The first person you went out with."

Instantly, the image of Jack, the sweet young painter Devon met within a week of moving to L.A., comes to mind. He was gentle and very educational, eager to teach an even more eager-to-learn Devon, who'd only had a couple of drunken hookups in college. He taught Devon what a relationship was like, and what Devon ultimately wanted: connection. But they parted, amicably enough, just too different to keep making it work. Devon smiles unwittingly, and thinks his name, keeping his mouth very carefully shut.

"Jack," Brandon says. "A painter?"

Fucking impossible. "You're a mind reader?"

Brandon laughs. "No. That's the thing. It's all you. Do you have any idea what you are?"

"What?" Devon pushes the drink farther away, feeling offended. *Do I know what I am?* "What the hell! What is that supposed to mean?"

"Look, do you need to test it more? I'll ask you more questions."

"No, just, tell me how you did that," Devon demands, and his stomach still wriggles. *God, what was in that drink?*

"I didn't, I'm trying to tell you," Brandon says. "You did it. You're projecting your thoughts. And you're doing it because of the drinks. They have mana in them."

"Mana?" Devon's stomach drops like a stone, then goes cold and very still. "Is it a drug? What did you give me—"

"It's not a drug. It's magic."

Devon's chest clenches, and suddenly it all clicks into focus. "Magic." *This guy is crazy. This whole place is one of those new-age crazy places with Tarot cards and crystals or something, and they've tricked me and are trying to scam me—*

"I haven't done Tarot a day in my life, okay? And I don't want anything from you. But you know I couldn't know that stuff, right?"

"No, you couldn't, unless, I don't know, but you're fucking with me—"

"I'm not—"

"Then something else—"

"Look, I can't convince you," Brandon says. "But I have someone who can. Can you just wait here for a second? I'll go get him." Brandon stands up. "Don't go anywhere! Drink your drink."

Devon doesn't touch his drink as Brandon heads over to the curtain and *knocks* on it as if it's made of wood. Devon blinks. He can't have seen that right; the curtain didn't even flutter. Maybe he just pretended to knock? But then the curtain does flutter, so Devon must have seen it wrong.

Brandon disappears behind the curtain. Devon toys with drinking the rest of his drink, but how can he know if they put something in it? That's the most likely explanation, even though he's pretty sure he kept his mouth shut. And really, how the hell did Brandon do that? Read his mind. *A reverse mind reader? Fuck that, that's ridiculous. There has to be another explanation.*

The curtain flutters again, and two people slip out. One is definitely a boy, but the other looks as though they'd rather you didn't try to guess their gender. *At least this place is inclusive.* The two giggle at each other and adjust their clothing. The area behind the curtain must be a private room. Devon wonders if this place caters to customers who like the performances a little too much.

They scamper off, and head to a door by the stage: backstage, likely. Devon watches them go, and then glances around the room. Mostly everyone has stopped staring at him, except for that damn front table again. Several of them still look at him. Devon gives a half smile, nods and then turns back around.

"Whoa."

The curtain is drawn back, now, on one side, as if it's a stage curtain, but beyond it is a simple continuation of the barroom, except that instead of tables, it has a single chair with a tiny table next to it. And standing next to Brandon, just outside the curtain, is a man.

He's tall, as tall as Brandon, but with jet black hair swept up off his face. He's got big blue eyes and a pert little nose, and freckles, so many freckles, on his pale skin. Devon half-expects his ears to be pointed, but they're normal ears. He wears leather pants and a tight, shimmering vest with faux fur around the collar. He's outrageous, and particularly striking. And his focus is right on Devon.

He ambles over casually, leaving Brandon to scurry back behind the bar. But Devon hardly notices him. Whoever-this-is stares at him and holds out a hand.

"I hear you're new here," the man says in a sweet voice. "I'm Eldan."

"Devon," Devon replies, shaking his hand.

"Oooh, a poet," Eldan replies, sinking sinuously onto the barstool beside Devon. "Do you know any good poems, Devon?"

"Songs, I guess," Devon replies. *A poet? Why would he assume that?*

Eldan grins. It scrunches his face up; it's very attractive. "I suppose that is poetry. So you're a musician?"

"I try to be," Devon says. "Are you, do you own this place?"

"I do," Eldan says. "Little ol' me."

Devon stares at him. "Okay. Um. Nice to meet you."

Eldan leans on a hand. "It's very nice to meet you, too. What brings you to my bar?"

Devon smiles. *This guy is pleasant and less awkward and weird than Brandon. And yeah, gorgeous too.* Devon can't look away. "I got lost and came in for directions. But Brandon keeps feeding me drinks and—uh— "

"Oh yes. That. I hear you need little ol' me to explain some things to you."

"Just one thing I guess," Devon says, steeling himself. *The guy's pretty, but that doesn't mean that things aren't fishy around here.* "How can Brandon hear my thoughts? Did you guys drug me?"

"Well, I suppose you could think of it like that, but mana is not a drug," Eldan says. "It's the essence of magic in this world. It flows in plants and streams and underground in ley lines. It's in our drinks, and if you drink them you get a temporary boost to your own natural stores of magic."

"So you're telling me I have magic in me?" Devon says, scoffing. "Yeah, right."

"Oh, you do," Eldan says. "And do you know why?"

"Wow. Okay. Why?"

Eldan stares at him.

"You're Fae."

ELDAN HAS LIVED LONG ENOUGH that he could have seen this city rise from the ground. But he didn't witness it firsthand; he only came to this place some forty years ago, though he wishes he could have seen how these people grew this city like weeds: pretty, smelly weeds, made of metal and gasoline and stone and wood. Eldan likes to see things grow, and he doesn't resent the humans' growth, even if it's in opposition to him and his kind. It's only natural.

Shame about the environment, of course, but the Earth will adapt. It might kill the humans in the process, which would also be a shame. But life will go on for Eldan, at least, if all goes well.

It's going *very* well currently. Though he was interrupted with his two sprite companions, his evening has been much improved by the presence of this intriguing changeling, Devon. Such a *young* man, too. Eldan feels old in comparison to his ignorance. Poor thing. He hardly knows anything about the world, *his* world, the world that was lost to him when he was raised by humans. But Eldan can bring him back to where he belongs.

"You're Fae."

Devon is, for all his youth, astoundingly attractive. Medium brown skin, certainly something elven in his features, lovely, deep brown eyes, stocky but strong build. Attractive, and Eldan senses *power* in him. Faint, but there, just waiting to be utilized. His thoughts trickle out, like leaves falling from trees—swishing, uncertain, weak, but bright and floating. Pieces of words and gestures of emotion, confusion and fear among them strongly, and attraction, of course. Eldan isn't surprised. There's a crackle between them, between their eyes, which don't seem to be able to look away from each other. Eldan could reach out and touch him. Would it spark?

Devon's angered frown is not so appealing, however. "Fae? Like, like faeries?"

"Yes, faeries are a type of Fae. I am one, and you most likely are as well, on top of being a changeling. But there are many types, as I'm sure you'll learn."

"You've gotta be kidding me."

"Would you like a demonstration, perhaps?" Eldan asks. He waves his right hand, and changes the heat at the core of his palm until a tiny, bright flash bursts in the air, quickly stifled and extinguished, but dazzling while it lasts. Like this man's thoughts, really.

Amazing, Eldan hears very clearly from Devon's mind. But Devon remains outwardly silent; his eyes are wide as he stares at Eldan's hand still held up before him.

"Would you like to see more?" Eldan asks.

"Yes," Devon says. "Tell me how you did that."

Eldan laughs. "I used magic. I channeled my mana into the molecules just above my palm. I used that energy to vibrate them against one another until they combusted. But without a better source of fuel, I can't keep the reaction going for more than the second without risking sending the club up in flames. Basically. Sort of."

"You're telling me it's magical science."

"Absolutely!" Eldan replies. "I'll tell you more about it some time. For now, do you understand that perhaps the world is bigger than you might have thought?"

Devon stares at him and then slowly nods. "Okay. Say I'm willing to open my mind to the possibility. You're telling me I'm Fae, whatever that means."

Eldan smiles; the edges of his mouth set hard. *A child, in so many ways, however beautiful he is.* "Whatever that means, indeed. It means a universe of life and light and magic that you have no means to comprehend yet. It means a family, a race, a species, that have lived long before and will live longer after everything else on this planet. It means a rich culture with its own government and religions and intrigues that you would require decades to properly study. It means an entire world you have yet to see. That's—*whatever.*"

Devon blinks. "I didn't mean any disrespect."

"And yet here we are," Eldan says, cocking his head. He pauses. "Do you believe me?"

"It's hard to," Devon says, "but it's hard not to. With the—the thing you did, and—"

"Easy," Eldan says, laying a hand on Devon's arm. It doesn't spark, but the buzz of energy is there. Eldan's hand feels *alive* where they connect. "One thing at a time."

Devon turns his attention to the room. Eldan realizes he's been so highly focused on this conversation that he has lost track of what's going on around them. It's not like him to get so caught up, but Devon is fascinating in his own way, and Eldan is very much drawn to him. And this conversation, like a catalyst, activates and revs up that natural attraction. Eldan is passionate about his people, and to have a newcomer, someone with whom he can discuss these things, is exciting.

Still, he shouldn't block out the world. That narrow focus isn't always welcomed by its recipients.

"Brandon," Eldan says, turning to the bar. Brandon wanders over from where he's been obviously eavesdropping and smiles. "Get us two shots of bri, will you?"

"What's *bri?*" Devon asks.

"Pure distilled alcohol made with mana," Eldan says. "Call it mana moonshine. It's the strongest dose of mana we have. I think it might ease you, and perhaps we can see more of these powers of yours."

"The—the mind stuff," Devon says.

"Oh yes."

"And maybe you can explain?" Devon says.

"Explain what? Everything? Where to even begin? How would you explain what it is to be human?"

Devon's brow furrows and his eyes drop and grow distant, and Eldan is pleased. Eldan can feel it coming from his mind, the important switch from confusion to curiosity.

Eldan finds him harder to resist by the moment, and now is not the time to make a move. The fact that Devon smells like wood smoke doesn't help.

"I guess I'd try to tell them what a human is," Devon finally says. "Like: We're animals, but we're the most intelligent life form we know of; we're the dominant life form? We have cities and various cultures and, yeah, I guess it's a lot to explain. I'd have to take the time to introduce someone to us bit by bit."

"Very well," Eldan says. "So what I can tell you now is that we are Fae. It's a title for all magically inclined creatures of the natural world. We are different from humans, absolutely, though most of us look similar and can even interbreed sometimes. But most of us don't dally. You, growing up as a human unknowing of your true self, would be a *changeling*, a simple faerie born to interbreed with the human race, to keep us alive."

"Keep you alive?"

"Ah, we do not adapt as humans do," Eldan explains. "Humans build and create technology and overcome the natural world. Fae are more in tune with the natural world, and move with it instead of against it. So we tend to stick to nature, most of us, that is. A few of us have made havens deep in the human world, so as to protect those of us who *do* choose to adapt our lifestyles, if not our magic—which we can't adapt."

"Like you?" Devon says. He's unwittingly eager, as though he can't help his curiosity. "Céilí is a haven. That's why you serve mana? Does it make magic easier?"

"You're smart. I am impressed. Yes, mana is natural magic. We take it mostly from ley lines, paths of magic that run in the earth. They tend to converge where cities grow. Los Angeles houses a massive ley line, as well as several smaller ones, which is why it's a natural place for a haven for Fae."

Eldan can hear Devon's mind sort through all the information he's been provided, can hear him compartmentalize and absorb. Just a tinge of disbelief remains. He seems to accept what Eldan says.

Finally, he settles on a question.

"So do you get like, trolls here?" Devon asks.

Eldan laughs. "No, not likely. Only Fae who can pass as human. Mostly faeries, like me and like you, some pixies, dwarves, that sort of thing. Trolls, humans would notice."

"They exist!?"

"Of course," Eldan says. "Many of your legends are based in some truth."

"What about dragons?"

Eldan laughs again. "Those we do not have. They perished long ago."

"You have to know," Devon says. "My mind is blown right now."

"So you finally believe."

"Just keep explaining. What do you do? If I reverse mind-read."

"You are a reverse empath, at the very least," Eldan says. "Do you find it easy to convince people of things?"

"Not lately," Devon says, bitter, bleak, even. Oh, that's a story for telling, sometime, Eldan is sure. Someone so young to be angry in this way.

"Ah, you feel left out, then?" Eldan guesses. "Like you never really fit in."

Devon stares up at him with his pretty, pretty eyes, and Eldan happily smiles into them while he awaits his answer.

"Yes," Devon says, finally. "Yes, I have felt like that. Like—I'm always one step off from everyone else."

"Yes, I imagine so. You'll find yourself much more at home here, I imagine."

"Here?" Devon asks. "In a bar?"

"We're more than a bar," Eldan says. "More than a burlesque show. More than a performance space. More than an apartment building and a restaurant, all of which we are. We're a *haven*. I have already told you this."

Devon sighs. "I'm sorry. It's a lot. And how the hell would I know what that means to you anyway, right?"

"I suppose. So you're forgiven," Eldan says. It's hard to stay mad at a pretty face. "And you're welcome here, if you wish." Devon flushes lightly, and Eldan smiles. "I mean it. You're one of us. All of our kind have a place here."

Devon doesn't seem capable of a reply. He takes a deep breath, and his mouth moves but no words come out. Finally, he rubs his face and shakes his head. "This is so much."

"I'm sorry for that," Eldan says. "It's hard to tell what information is essential right off the bat, and I err on the side of too much over too little."

"No, it's—it's good; I want to know things. But I could use that drink, right about now."

Eldan glances up; Brandon stands off to one side, holding the two full shot glasses. "Yeah, been here a while now," he says. "Want these?"

"You could very well have set those down, Brandon," Eldan says, a little miffed.

"You looked busy." Brandon grins. "On the house?"

"On the house indeed," Eldan says as he takes his shot glass. *On the house.* He's the goddamn owner, everything is on the house at all times. He pays enough for it. He turns back to Devon. "Ignore him." He smiles and then says, "Pay attention to me instead."

Devon is startled enough to laugh as he takes his shot glass and holds it up. "Oh, wow."

Eldan grins. "*Sláinte.* Drink up."

Eldan tosses back his shot. He isn't a fan of bri most days. It's far too bitter; he prefers mixed drinks, but for tonight he'll drink in solidarity as Devon takes his own shot. It's the quickest way to test this man's powers, after all.

And it works. As soon as the drink hits Devon's stomach, mana flows into Devon's body without a need for veins, flowing instead through the channels of energy within his body, which flow through his blood vessels and organs. In just a few moments, his energy heightens, and Eldan can hear all his surface thoughts.

A mind is not like a book to be read. It's a confusing mess most of the time, with words and emotions and distractions and memories and reactions all mixed in one big jumble. So Eldan has to do his best to pick out what Devon's untrained mind is allowing to mix together. It's like trying to pick out ingredients while watching a blender in action.

But oh, Eldan is glad to feel attraction from Devon's mind. Attraction, curiosity, excitement, that tinge of doubt, still. He's in an overall good frame of mind; that much Eldan can tell. Weary, though; everything moves a little slower than expected. Perhaps it's best not to put any more information into that mind for the time being.

"Would you like to watch a performance with me?" Eldan asks. "We have a singer coming on in just a moment."

The truth is, Eldan simply wants to keep talking to Devon, keep connecting with him. He's fascinating. Eldan hasn't talked to a changeling for quite some time, and never one so new.

Eldan can't help listening in. Devon is open. He's as open as anyone Eldan has met. Everything is right there on the surface. Not that he has no depth, but he has no *secrets*; he's not hiding anything. Or if he is, Eldan can't guess what it might be. But all his thoughts slide through his mind like water babbling over stones, and not a whirlpool or crevice to be found. No sudden dropping of ideas, no silenced trains of thought, just a simple, smooth glide from one idea to the next, natural and easy. Of course, Devon's never been trained to keep his mind a secret. In his world, the mind *is* secretive, and he can choose what people hear or don't hear. Eldan will have to train him to keep secrets and he will have to shield the thoughts Devon can't help in the meantime. Now, however, Devon doesn't seem to *mind* Eldan hearing him, so he can take advantage of that, right?

Devon turns to him and his thoughts turn sharply to focus on Eldan.

"You didn't tell me what your powers are."

How much he can divulge? Best not to overwhelm him, he's already decided that. But still, Eldan doesn't *know* this man; perhaps he shouldn't lay it all on the table.

"I control matter," Eldan says. "Atoms. I can freeze water and melt ice. I can start a flame or extinguish a blaze. As long as there are atoms to manipulate, I can manipulate them."

"Can all Fae do that?"

"No. Fae have various powers that they prefer. I mean, with enough study, you can manipulate your magic any way you please, but we all have special talents. I am very good at micromanaging, I suppose you could say. You, you can project your thoughts. And with training, you could control your powers and do even more than that. You may very well be able to make people think your thoughts as though they were their own. You could get into the minds of others. You could even control people's minds, if you went the distance and had enough power. Quite a tool of manipulation. Frightening, perhaps."

"But I wouldn't—"

"Oh, don't underestimate yourself," Eldan says. "Think with some subtlety. You could simply *nudge* someone to like you. You could influence them to agree with your point of view. You could be a fantastic politician."

"Not my strong suit, I'm afraid," Devon says, and Eldan senses his mind whirling with anxiety. "I'm just a musician."

His discomfort is anything but pleasant, and Eldan strokes his shoulder to settle him.

"Easy," he says. "Be easy. You don't have to do anything you don't want to do. But imagine. What if you could really make people *feel* your music? You could make any audience love you. You could get any record label to sign you. You could set your own salary and record the songs *you* want to record. You could *own* the music industry."

Devon's eyes widen, and for a long moment, they meet Eldan's and *connect*. "I—I guess you're right."

"You could do *wonderful* things, Devon," Eldan says. "You have that power."

"It's not as impressive as yours."

"Everyone's different," Eldan says, smug. After all, atomic manipulation *is* pretty impressive. Not that he'll say that out loud.

"Well…. Oh, the performance." Devon looks up to the stage as the music starts. "Should I watch? Isn't that what we're doing?"

"You might not enjoy this number," Eldan says, as Maia takes the stage. "And I'm certain it's not aimed at you anyway."

"Aimed at me?"

"Maia is a succubus," Eldan explains. "But she's only interested in her own kind."

"Succubuses—or is it succubi?"

Eldan laughs. "I mean women."

Devon nods and smiles as Maia dances and sings. She's average height, with dark, wavy hair and a severe, but very pretty, face. She's wearing black shorts and a crop top, so her smooth brown skin is revealed. She's in the center of the stage, just her and a microphone, while backup dancers twirl behind her. The women in the audience, along with most of the men, seem enraptured, but Devon's thoughts drift free of her influence. He turns back to Eldan, body and mind.

"Thanks for the drinks, by the way," Devon says with a shy smile. Oh, how is Eldan supposed to resist this? He's gorgeous, he's open, he's attractive in more ways than one. Eldan succumbs to his pull, his own brand of charisma, that dark mysterious quality in him that isn't dented even by his openness. How does he manage? It's the eyes; his eyes look as though they hold secrets. As though there's so much more to him than Eldan has seen. And of course there is; he's a person, he has endless depths. Eldan wants to plumb those depths. He's a romantic. Or not so romantic, if he wants to take it the euphemistic way.

Perhaps he might be the *one*, after all. No telling until some connection is made, and they did have several *moments* together: moments when Eldan heard Devon think of Eldan as *gorgeous* and moments when Eldan felt them *understanding* each other through their curiosities—he can sense the understanding in Devon and in himself. Devon is attractive and attracted to Eldan. They are both warm-blooded males, loose with drink. Perhaps more can happen.

"Would you stay?" Eldan asks. "We have rooms. Or you could stay with me."

Devon coughs, holding his drink away from himself. "I—wow."

"Was I too forward?" Eldan asks. "I saw no reason to deny my interest."

"I think, maybe, yes," Devon says. "I'm not really interested in, you know. What you were doing before."

Eldan is confused, but then Devon's thoughts make his meaning perfectly clear: the sprites, stumbling out of his office earlier, and suspicions about what he had done with them. What does that matter? Eldan hadn't done anything with them. Does Devon think he'd be required to have others join them? Or is he simply jealous?

"Simple dalliance," Eldan says, guessing the latter.

"Exactly," Devon says. "I don't *do* that."

Eldan can *feel* Devon's disgust, his disdain. He sighs and resumes. "Our culture does not condemn sex as yours does."

"I don't think sex is condemnable," Devon says. He thinks, *I just don't throw myself around.*

That stings. Devon finds him *distasteful.* The connection between them, which had been strong, *potential,* something big and hopeful for Eldan, is lost, and Eldan draws back. Mate potential, really, and Eldan only wished to see if their spark was what it seemed. But Devon finds him distasteful? He's not *throwing himself around.* He's *searching.*

"Very well," he says. "If that is your wish, I will refrain from pressuring you."

Devon notices that he's upset Eldan and he grimaces. "I'm sorry. You're— you're lovely; I just don't like one night stands."

"I quite understand," Eldan says. There's no point holding onto the offense, as much as it rankles. Still, the mood is ruined, the connection severed. "I suppose you would like to leave now?" Devon takes it as a dismissal, and Eldan sighs. "You may stay if you wish. We have empty apartments," Eldan adds.

"No," Devon says. "I should go home and think about all of this. I should think about it with a *clear head.*"

He's not entirely sober, and Eldan nods. "I'll have Brandon call you a cab."

"I can't afford a cab," Devon says, and Eldan is surprised. So easy to admit that? Perhaps he *is* quite drunk. Or is he even more open than Eldan had thought?

"I'll take care of it," Eldan says. "Look, take our number and call, won't you?" Eldan stands with Devon and holds his gaze. "No matter what, you are one of us, Devon. This is where you belong."

Devon's thoughts whir. Eldan pulls his own mind back, shielding against him. It's time for privacy; he should have been shielding long before. He's simply been *curious,* drawn to Devon's thoughts like a moth to flame or a beast to water.

"I'll think about it," Devon says.

"Brandon." Brandon comes when he's called, and Eldan says, "Call him a cab and pay for it ahead of time. Then give him our number."

Brandon scribbles on a napkin and then uses his cell to order a taxi. Devon stands awkwardly, and Eldan no longer can hear his thoughts clearly, so he just cocks his head at Devon. The mana has worn off enough to make things quieter.

"I hope we'll see you soon," he says, and then he takes Devon's hand and kisses it. "Genuinely."

Then he goes to the head table, where his people sit. His crew, his *family*. Kelsi welcomes him by grabbing his hand and smiling up at him. Eldan swings their hands.

Eldan keeps his eyes on the room as Maia's performance comes to an end. The crowd is restless, and whispers circulate. What about? Devon, perhaps?

Kelsi tugs on his hand and swivels to face him. Eldan smiles down at her and says, "Yes, pet?"

"Just wondering what you two were talking about at the end. I couldn't eavesdrop after he stopped projecting."

"When did he stop projecting?" Eldan asks. He drops his shields and checks. He can't hear Devon anymore. He isn't inside anymore, and neither is Brandon. "I heard him fine until a few moments ago, when I shielded."

"Hm," Kelsi says. "Maybe because you were right next to him?"

"Perhaps," Eldan says, considering the possibilities. "We'll simply have to see."

3

THE NEXT MORNING, DEVON'S MOUTH tastes like glue. Like white, sticky, schoolhouse glue. Like the old, stale, flaky sticky half-used glue round the top of the nozzle. Like *really really gross.*

He should definitely brush his teeth.

After taking his medication he washes his face, washes his hair, takes a shower. He shaves with an electric razor, not too close; the scruffy look is good on him. He needs a haircut, maybe. A short fade would be good, but he doesn't want to spend the money. He could set his razor to shave close and pray he shaves evenly. It would be fast and cheap, and it doesn't look *awful* that way.

But he doesn't have the energy to shave his head.

The night before is a strange memory, in the way that drunken memories often are: distorted, as if he might not have been seeing things the way they really were, as though his perception was different than it would be now. That makes sense, given the whole alcohol thing.

What would he see if he wandered exactly as he wandered last night, ending up at Céilí? Would he walk in, see beautiful Eldan in his tall, slender paleness, his black hair and his freckles and his blue, blue, blue eyes? Would he see the magic Eldan performed, so *cool* but so unbelievable, even right in front of his eyes?

Would he see himself there? That's what he was told he had *found.* That's what matters.

You're Fae, they said. They said *a lot.* Most of it, Devon remembers. But most of it is still mixed up and faded even after just one night. The memories nag at Devon all the while he gets ready for his weekend job driving the forklift at the supermarket.

Maybe someone slipped something in his drink before they gave it to him, or when he was distracted with Brandon. That would make sense. He hallucinated part of the time, and the rest of the time they played a prank on him. He went to a club with a sick sense of humor and a drug habit. He got played, that's all.

The nagging doesn't go away, so he discards that hypothesis by the time his shift is finished. But what does that mean? Is he really not, not *human*? Can he use magic to put his thoughts in other people's heads? And that means, that means he's not his parents' child, unless one of them is Fae, too.

But that's the answer. He needs to call his parents and ask them what they know. They might think he's crazy, but it will settle this. Then he can safely attribute the churning in his gut to a hangover as any sane person would.

He makes the call as soon as he gets home.

"Hello, there," his father says, in his Northern Irish accent.

"Hey, Dad," Devon says. "Mom there?"

"She's changing. Need her?"

"Just nearby?" Devon says. "I don't know how to ask this."

"Something wrong?"

"Maybe?"

"Well, tell us."

Devon sighs. He might as well rule out the adoption theory before asking his parents if one of them is a magical creature. "This is going to sound crazy. But, um, am I adopted?"

Silence. Devon checks the line: still live, but his father remains speechless. Dread fills him, instant and cold. "Dad?"

"I think your mother should take this, son. Give us a sec."

Devon goes completely cold. He sits on the edge of his bed and breathes slowly and steadily to stave off the rising nausea. *God. Could it be true?*

"Devon?"

His mother's softer, lilting voice comes on the line.

"Mom?"

"Your father says you've something to ask me."

"Yeah. I need to know if—Am I adopted? Or—" He lets it hang.

"Oh, Devon. What makes you think that?"

"Just answer, Mom."

"Oh my love. It's complicated."

"Oh my god," Devon says. "I'm, it's true. It's fucking true."

"What have you been told?"

"Does it matter?" Devon asks. His chest hurts. "I'm, I'm not your son. I'm not your son."

The world shatters around him, and tears fill his eyes. His mother, his father, they're not his parents. Every hug, every *I love you*, rare as they were, and more precious for it, they were all lies. He doesn't know who he *is*.

"Yes, you are," his mother insists. "You *are* my son. I didn't birth you, that's true, but you've been mine from the moment you started breathing, that I know."

"Who am I?" Devon sobs. "God, Mom—"

"I know, poor boy. I know, I'm so sorry we didn't tell you. But it never was the right time, was it?"

"Who am I, Mom? Where did you get me?"

"It's a long story, one I'd rather tell in person," his mother says. "But, you were given to us by an *angel*."

"An angel?"

"My mother called them *aes sidhe*," his mother says. "This one told me to call her Macha. She birthed you and laid you on our doorstep."

"Why?"

"Because I asked for you. I prayed to every god I knew for you, and one of them answered. That's all you need to know now. I *wanted* you so much that I wished you into being, and you were given to me. That's what matters."

"It matters to me, Mother," Devon says, anger growing in him alongside the devastation. "You've lied to me for my *entire life*. How could you?"

"And how would I tell you? 'Dear son, I prayed for you and you arrived on a doorstep. Surprise, you were never in my womb?' Because that's the only way you are not my boy. I didn't give you birth but I gave you life."

I gave you life. Something about that hits Devon, and all the little moments, all the love, however little it was shown, comes back to him. No, she's not his birth mother, but she's his *mom*. She raised him, however seldom she was around. His dad, too.

But he can't face what her statement means right now. Not like this.

"I want to hear the whole story," he says. "When can you come visit?"

"Not right now. I've got too much work. The files for the case I'm working on are due tomorrow, and I've got another case just starting. I suppose you won't come here?"

Of course she'd put it on him. He'd tried to reach out to them his entire life and he got nothing in return but *I've got too much work*. She works with shelter kids as a caseworker, and she could never turn her focus from them onto her own kid. And his father was always off on weird hours with the trains.

"Why, Mom?" Devon asks. "Why have me? You were barely around."

His mother is silent for a moment. "I wanted you for myself. I overestimated my own abilities. But I still had you; you were still mine."

"But you weren't *mine*," Devon says.

She sighs. "Come visit. We need to talk about this in person."

Well, he's not going to step out of his way. "I can't afford it, Mom."

"I'll pay—"

"No. You know I won't. We'll just have to wait till there's time or money."

"We'll see. But, now you know. There it is."

Devon nods. "There it is. I have to go."

"One question, Devon. How did you find out?"

Devon licks his lips, considering, but there's no time. Not now that he knows.

"I'll tell you when I visit," he says. "I think I'll know better then."

Silence, and then his mother says, "So be it. Call next week?"

"Sure," Devon says. "I will."

"Goodbye, darling."

As he hangs up, a sense of total loss washes over Devon. He drops his phone to the bed and buries his head in his hands, trying to breathe. His parents aren't really his parents. Some strange woman dropped him on a porch. His whole *identity* is a question. And maybe this is why his parents never loved him enough, because he wasn't really theirs, was he? Maybe they wanted a baby badly enough, but they got tired of him, despite what his mother said. And who was that woman? Why did she give him up? How did she find his—the people who took him, became his family? Who's his biological father? What race is he, what illnesses run in his family, who gave him his eye color, what—

God, is he what they said? Is he what his mother's mother would say? Is he—

Does the label matter? He's not who he thought he was.

And now he has to get ready for his second job, another one he can barely stand: serving drinks at a trendy little club, barely scraping tips, ending the night smelling like alcohol and sweat and not in the fun way. It's hours of running back and forth, taking orders, filling orders, waiting for the already-busy bartenders, getting sneered at by people with more money and more style than he, tripping over himself to be attractive and attentive and smiley and friendly in hopes of not being stiffed.

He stands up, and every muscle in his body resists. It's as if he's suddenly filled with lead instead of blood, as if gravity has increased. Why on earth is he putting himself through this?

There's no more reason in the world. He's not who he thought he was. How he defined himself has suddenly revealed itself to be no more than a veil, flimsy and thin and fragile. It has hidden who he really was all along, and who he really is. God, he has to discover that all over again. Twenty-four years of being, all for nothing.

And it's not as if much was there to lose. He's a failed musician, a two-job chump who can barely make the bills. He's got no close friends; his family is a *lie*. His relationships have all faded into nothing. They weren't even passionate enough to blow up at the end. They flickered out, puff, a wisp of smoke and gone. He's left no impression on this world; he's nothing special. And he has no plan going forward.

The frustration with his life coalesces in his gut like a boiling cauldron. The heat writhes and rises, until it fills his eyes with tears and colors them red. His hands move of their own volition. He stands, and suddenly his lamp is broken against the wall. He has a memory of throwing it, but not of control. Shames rushes in, and he unplugs the lamp before it starts sparking.

There. He ruined something he paid money for, and guilt easily joins the anger, the desolation.

He might as well disappear, because he doesn't *belong* anywhere.

This is where you belong.

Eldan told him he belonged at Céilí. Could that be true? Could Devon live in that world?

Could he learn what it is to be Fae? Could he learn something about his past, the past that started long before he was born? Could he find his birth mother? Does he want to find someone who gave him up so easily, who might have had him only to fulfill Mom's wishes? Could he, could he find somewhere to be himself? Eldan offered to accept him. And screw it, he really wants that. He's always wanted that.

Devon leaps up and heads to his clothes hamper. Right on top are the jeans he wore last night; Devon reaches into the pockets and roots until he finds a slip of paper.

Céilí. 213-555-0303.

Work can wait, or go fuck itself entirely. Devon doesn't care. All he can do is pull out his phone and dial.

He's not certain whether he wants someone to pick up, because it might be Eldan on the other end of the line.

Ring. Ring. Devon is quite confused as to his feelings about Eldan. On one hand, he offended the guy; he might as well have called him a slut and been done with it. On the other hand, Devon is fascinated by him, by what he represents, his authority and his knowledge in the Fae world. He wants to talk to Eldan, get to know him. And then, the guy is gorgeous, and Devon's not blind. No matter his own mores regarding the matter, part of him wants to lie back and let Eldan play with his body and just enjoy. But that's not who he is. Devon can control himself perfectly well, thank you. Too bad that he has to—he'd love to get to know Eldan in other circumstances—but he can.

Ring.

"Hello?"

"Hi," Devon says to the female voice. "Um. My name's Devon?"

"Is it?" the voice says. "Hold on."

Silence, and then a rustle, until, "Devon. You called." It's Eldan.

"Yes," Devon says. "I did."

"Interested in a one-nighter after all, are we?"

Devon blinks. "No? I just—"

Eldan laughs heartily. "No, of course not, darling. I was joking. Please, by all means, what can I help you with?"

Devon's mind goes completely blank. What on earth had driven him to call? "Um?"

"I can't actually hear your mind over the line, Devon, so you'll have to speak up."

"Sorry," Devon says. He slaps his head and then he remembers. "Oh. I, I talked to my parents."

"Yes?"

"They, uh, they confirmed. What you said."

"I'm so sorry, love," Eldan says. "I know this must be difficult for you."

That hits Devon right in his chest—he rubs there unconsciously and nods his head as if Eldan can see him. "Yeah. I guess."

"Look, why don't you drop by? We can talk more."

"I have to get to work," Devon says.

"Tomorrow, then. Or whenever you're free. We'll always be here."

Devon considers his schedule. "I can come over tomorrow afternoon."

"Do. We'd all like to see you."

"Where are you? I don't quite remember."

"Ah. Well. Do you know Century City?"

"Vaguely," Devon says.

"Head down Century Park West and you'll find us. Just follow your heart."

Devon can't tell if this is a joke, and laughing seems rude if it isn't, so he says, "Okay. I'll see you tomorrow afternoon."

"We will without a doubt be here. Have a good night at work. Oh, speaking of which, I have a little experiment for you. How would you feel about that?"

"I guess it depends," Devon says. His heart quickens with the possibilities. Experiment? What kind? What will he be doing? Will Eldan be involved?

"Tonight, try to push a thought onto someone else. Ask them for a bigger tip, perhaps? Simply slip that thought into someone's mind."

"How?"

"Imagine a thread between your mind and theirs and send the message down the line. It's a simple enough trick for someone with your talents; let's see if you can manage it."

"I can, I can try," Devon says.

"Ah. So your morals don't extend to conning, then. Just sex? Good to know. We'll be seeing you!"

Click. Fucking—what did he just say? Devon doesn't know how to take what was said. A gentle tease from a new friend? A slight from a jilted playboy? An outright insult to his character? Either way, Devon's anger rises for the second time that day. How dare he?

He pockets his cell, stands up and checks himself over. He appears to be fine. He's angry but less confused, and now he can go into work at least. He's late, but he can come up with an excuse on the way in.

Family emergency, he thinks, heading out the door. *I've lost my parents.*

THE NEXT DAY, DEVON LEAVES his house with a pocket full of the ample tips he made the night before and a totally different attitude. For one, he's feeling expansive enough to order a cab to where he's going. For another, he's no longer angry, because the experiment *worked*.

All night he got nothing but large tips. He got more than the usual buck or two all night and from plenty of people. Even after splitting tips at the end of the night, he went home with a hefty bundle of bills. He heads to his other job with the money securely in his wallet, which is tucked in his extremely tight back pocket, and all through the day he keeps checking to make sure it is still there. He's not used to having this much money.

After he goes home and washes off the sweat and changes his clothes, he heads out for his cab with a spring in his step. The cabbie ignores him, of course, but it doesn't matter.

Century City is new and fresh when he gets out of the cab halfway up Century Park West, but it's also familiar. He recognizes this street. He gets his bearings and heads up the road.

And there it is: a factory building, brick and wavy glass, roughly square, big. Céilí. It looks different in the daylight, but it's exactly where he left it. The sign is lit and the doors aren't locked. So he slides in, first one door and then the second, until he's faced with the interior of Céilí.

It's well-lit and mostly empty but for one full table near the bar. Six of the eight chairs around it are taken up. Devon picks out Brandon, Kelsi and Eldan. The others spare him a glance, but those three smile and wave.

"Come," Eldan calls. "We've been waiting."

Devon smiles uncertainly and heads over with his eyes on the two free chairs: one next to Eldan and Kelsi, and one between Brandon and a slight girl. He breathes a sigh of relief that the closest one is next to Brandon. Devon isn't sure he could handle being too close to Eldan without feeling awkward.

"Hey, man," Brandon says as Devon sits. "Want some coffee?"

"Yeah, sure. Thanks."

Brandon grabs a cup from the center of the table and pours from a ceramic carafe. The coffee's aroma wafts up; it's too strong for Devon's taste, so he grabs a few of the little creamers that sit next to the remaining empty cups, along with some sugar packets.

"So, I don't know everyone," Devon says, preparing his coffee. "I'm Devon."

"We know," the slight girl to his right says. "I'm Serena."

"The pixie," Eldan says. "She runs the distillery downstairs."

Serena grins. Her teeth are very tiny, like the rest of her. "That's me."

"This is Maia," Eldan says, nodding to the woman on his left. "You saw her perform the other night."

Devon glances at her. She's different in the light of day, but yes, she's familiar. She wears a lot less makeup, and her skin is sallow and almost dirty. Devon smiles at her. "Hi."

"Uh huh," she replies. Devon blinks.

"Ignore her," Eldan says. "She didn't get to eat last night and she's simply starving, aren't you darling?"

"Not my fault we're overbooked," Maia says acidly, staring Eldan down. "Some of us need an attentive audience, not to share the stage."

"We have to make room for everyone, Maia," Eldan says. "Some of us don't have day jobs to rely on. Speaking of which, shouldn't you be going? You'll be able to feed when you do."

"Yeah," she says. "Fine. I have to get ready."

"Go," Eldan says. "Get yourself glamorous so you can feed on the needy young women of this city." He glances at Devon and winks.

Next to him, Serena speaks up. "She's a professional dominatrix by day. A good job for a pretty young succubus."

"I'm eighty-three years old," Maia snaps. "Knock it off."

"You don't look a day over twenty, my dear," Eldan says, kissing her cheek. She rolls her eyes, but doesn't look displeased. And Devon can only agree; she could be younger than he is. *Eighty three?*

"Oh yes," Eldan says. "Most of us are older than we look, except for Brandon; he's a changeling like you, only thirty years old. A child among wolves," he adds with an appropriately wolfish grin.

"Harr, harr," Brandon says. "I can hold my own, old man."

"So. Did you find us all right?" Eldan asks.

"Yeah," Devon replies. "Speaking of which, how come people don't just come in all the time? It's right there."

"Cloaking spells," Eldan says. "Glamours. It looks like a construction site, but nothing ever gets constructed. Perfect cover: No one comes in; no one has the urge to come in. We are perfectly ignorable."

Like Harry Potter, Devon thinks, and Eldan laughs.

"A little," he says.

"Wait." Devon's eyes sweep around at everyone. "I didn't say anything out loud."

Everyone at the table smiles. Eldan smiles the widest and says, "That's because we spiked the coffee."

Devon puts down his cup and pushes it away. "You did drug me, didn't you?" he asks.

"Never," Eldan says. "Just a touch of bri. Not even enough to affect your sobriety very much; we only wanted to test your powers. And teach you a little something."

He stands and circles the table, ending up right behind Devon. He places his hands on Devon's shoulders and leans down. "Now, I want you to imagine an impenetrable bubble around your mind. Build it out of the strongest material you know. And imagine your thoughts safe inside, and the rest of us stuck outside of it. Because we're all able hear everything you think."

He presses his lips against Devon's ear.

"What are you doing?" Devon asks.

"Telling you secrets," Eldan says. "Like how I wanted so badly for you to come to my rooms with me when I met you. Could you tell? Could you see that I wanted to lay you out on my bed and take you apart?"

Fuck. His hands are strong on Devon's shoulders and there's something about Eldan that he can't shake. His mind can only run amok with the provided imagery. But everyone can hear, everyone can see—

A bubble. An impenetrable bubble. He closes his eyes and pictures it as Eldan continues to whisper.

"I wanted to kiss your pretty mouth, Devon. I wanted to put my hands on your body and undress you bit by bit. Would've put my mouth everywhere. Would've teased you till you were begging for it. Would've opened you up and fucked you like you deserve to be fucked—long and slow, except when I couldn't stop myself. Then it would be hard, right until you needed to come. But I'd make you wait."

A *shield.* Made of iron, locked and riveted around his brain, metal plates around the inside of his skull. Electrically charged iron, to keep *everything* out.

"And when I had you sobbing for it," Eldan charges on, his lips moving against Devon's ear, and his fingers questing, digging little lines into the muscles of Devon's heaving chest, "I'd finally give it to you how you wanted, finally fuck you right into the mattress, hold you down and let you come around my cock."

"Are you going to stop?" Brandon asks. "We all have places to be."

"I'll stop when he shields," Eldan says.

"He *is* shielding," Kelsi says.

Eldan pulls back, and Devon sags in relief. His shield *works.* It keeps people *out,* and he suddenly feels much safer. It might not be perfect, but he can *do* it—

But why did Eldan keep going? Devon holds the image of the shield in his mind and it's solid. No one is paying him attention; they're all looking at Eldan. So they all can't hear his frantic thoughts.

No one but Eldan. Devon catches his eye and very deliberately thinks, *Can you still hear me?*

Eldan nods his head the tiniest bit as he sidles away, and Devon's heart clenches in his chest. *How?*

"Congratulations, anyway," Brandon says. "We got to something about begging before it cut out. Good job, man."

"Very good," Kelsi says. "You learn fast."

"He's still got a lot to learn," Eldan says. "Devon, why don't you and I take a walk and talk some more. We can let the rest of these miscreants get to their business."

Everyone stands up. Devon wishes he could have more coffee, spiked and all. But he ignores his cup and walks over to Eldan, who is speaking in a low voice to Kelsi.

"—hopefully you can bring her by sometime," he's saying. "We have room for more, as you can see."

"Not yet," Kelsi says. "She's a human, you know? And I don't know for sure yet."

"I say you'll be officially mated within six months," Eldan says, smiling. Kelsi returns the smile, shaking her head.

"Maybe." She turns to Devon. "We haven't been officially introduced."

"Devon," Devon says, holding out his hand. Kelsi takes it in a strong hand.

"Kelsi," she says. "I'm the bouncer and sometimes-bartender."

She bears herself like an athlete; her dark limbs are long and strong.

"I bet you could throw me out if you wanted."

"I could," she says.

Eldan laughs. "She could throw you three blocks away if she wanted. Stay on her good side. Which shouldn't be hard; she doesn't *have* a bad side."

"You're my bad side," she says, and Eldan laughs again. "I need you to fix my leg, by the way—the cup is uncomfortable again."

"We can take care of it now," Eldan says. "Devon, would you mind?"

"No," he says. "I'm just here. I don't need anything."

"It'll be but a moment," Eldan says. "But you should watch and—Kelsi, would you mind if I turned this into another lesson?"

"Go ahead," she says, sitting down and hiking up her loose pants, revealing a prosthetic leg. "But don't fuck up what you're doing, please? It's uncomfortable enough."

"I will be as gentle as possible should I need to manipulate your tissue again," Eldan says. "Just relax. Devon, stand by Kelsi please?"

Devon sidles next to her, and Eldan smiles up at him.

"Now," he says, putting his hands on Kelsi's prosthetic near the knee. "I need to adjust the shape of the socket to bear the weight better. We're working with less technologically advanced gadgetry with this older model; it doesn't have a computer to adjust weight-bearing, so we're going to do that on our own. After I do that, I'll adjust the shape of the scar tissue at the bottom of her thigh to be more comfortable, and that can be uncomfortable for Kelsi. I'd like you to distract her."

"How?" Devon asks.

"I want you to try to project a thought into her mind," Eldan says. "Drop your shield to do so. In due course you'll learn to keep it up *and* project at the same time. But for now, Kelsi won't take advantage of your vulnerability, will you my dear?"

"Go ahead," Kelsi says. "Gimme what you got."

"I want you to picture a calming place," Eldan says. "Perhaps a forest, or a river, or a cave. Somewhere pleasant and peaceful. And I want you to imagine that image flowing from your mind into Kelsi's. Like a thread, like I told you last night. Can you try to do that for me?"

"I can try," Devon says. "Um. I feel stupid doing this."

"Yes, I imagine this is out of your comfort zone," Eldan says. "But why don't you try."

"Um—sure." Devon turns to Kelsi. "Ready?"

Kelsi nods, and Devon puts a hand on her shoulder. Then, he gazes into her eyes, and tries to push the image of a forest into her mind. It's a lot more difficult than a simple *tip large* thought; he has to craft a whole image in his head and hold onto it while he sends it to her. And nothing happens.

He feels like an idiot. He's got the image of the forest and he imagines it flows from him to her, but she just stares at him expectantly.

"Nothing?" he asks.

"Nothing yet," she says, and then winces. "Careful, Eldan."

"Apologies," he says. "We'll be done soon. Devon, please continue."

"But it's not doing anything," he says, trying hard to force the forest out of his head and into Kelsi's. He imagines a string of thought out from his eyes and into hers, but she shakes her head and winces. "This is ridiculous."

"Well, I'm done," Eldan says. "How does it feel, Kelsi?"

Kelsi stands next to Devon and tests her weight. "Better than before. But I might have to see if I can get a new one."

"Will the government pay for it?" Eldan asks. "Or should we start fundraising?"

"I'll talk to the VA rep," she says. "Thanks for doing what you can. And thanks for trying, Devon. You'll get it eventually."

"At least you'll be ready for your date tonight, hmm?" Eldan says.

"Hopefully," Kelsi says. She nods to Devon. "I'll see you later?"

"Yeah," Devon says, smiling at her. She leaves, and he is alone with Eldan.

Eldan has been nothing but welcoming and informative and attentive, maybe too attentive. But Devon may have overreacted. Eldan didn't pressure him; he took Devon's *no* with impressive grace, though he seemed put out. Devon's thoughts were revealed, and he couldn't hide his dislike of the lifestyle Eldan had shown himself to lead. Eldan can live as he likes, but Devon hates one night stands. He had enough of them in college, when seeking deeper connection and being thrown out in the morning hurt too much. Ever since, he has been a relationship guy.

But he was uncharitable the other night and he should apologize. Eldan doesn't seem to expect it; he just smiles and raises an eyebrow at Devon.

"So. Shall we talk?"

Eldan nods and walks away.

Devon follows him, winding around the bar and behind it, to a door that leads into an industrial-sized kitchen.

"We serve dinner here, too," Eldan says. "As well as feeding everyone who lives here regularly."

"How do you keep hidden?" Devon asks, as they head up a staircase at the back of the kitchen. "You said you had spells, but what about electricity? Do you run on magic?"

"Absolutely not. There are better uses for our magic, and we don't have an unlimited supply. No, we use the city's power and its water, and we pay for all of it. The spells shield us from those who wonder why an unused construction site needs electricity."

At the top of the stairs, they turn down a long, straight hallway with doors on either side every forty feet or so. Eldan walks right to the end, to a door on the right. Devon sees a door across the hall and a door at the very end of the hall, which doesn't have a handle, just a lock.

"What—"

"Here." Eldan opens the door on the right. "Have a look."

Devon enters the room and finds himself in a large loft space. It's a hipster's dream: all exposed brick and plaster, hardwood floors and wavy glass windows from floor to ceiling around two walls to the left and front. A small living area holds a mismatched couch and chairs, and a little kitchen occupies one corner. Just to the right ahead of him, a door opens to a bathroom, and on his immediate right is an open door to what seems to be a dark bedroom.

"Holy shit," Devon says, surveying all of it. "Whose place is this?"

Eldan lifts his arm and lays his elbow on Devon's shoulder. "Yours. If you want it."

The breath rushes from Devon's chest and leaves him achingly empty. "Mine?"

"Yours."

He breathes in again, and the emptiness is filled. They really want him here?

"We do," Eldan says aloud. "You're one of us. And we have to take care of our own. There are few enough of us as it is, out here in the wasteland."

Devon quirks a smile. "I'd hardly call L.A. a wasteland."

"Oh, but it is," Eldan says. "Our kind are made to be in forests and glens and mountains and cliffs, in the jungles and the seas, even in the desert. We live in nature; we connect with its magic." Eldan sighs. "There's so little magic left. When humans take over, it dies. All natural life is cut off, and the cycles stop. We're making do on a ley line here, otherwise there wouldn't be enough mana. This is deep Earth magic. We can't do any other kind. This land is—barren."

Eldan drops his arm and takes Devon's hand with a smile. He leads him to the couch, sits and pats the seat beside him. Devon sits.

"So—why stay here? If it's a wasteland."

Eldan shrugs. "It's a good wasteland. We survive. And the Fae need a place to call their own, you know. We *need* a haven. In the midst of all this, Céilí is an oasis. You don't need an oasis in the middle of verdant growth, do you?"

"No," Devon says. "You need it in the desert."

"Exactly," Eldan says. "Don't those of us on the outskirts of our society deserve a safe place as well?"

Devon blinks. "Well… yes."

Eldan smiles and settles back, turned toward Devon. "Céilí is the only professionally run haven in the United States, and one of two in the entire Western Hemisphere. Sure, there are small places here and there, but I supply hundreds of patrons every week. That's not much to you, who have lived in the human world and seen its countless thousands, but it's huge to us. Few of us are left; most of us are still over in the Old Land. The Court and our Queens remain in Summerland. And to go to Summerland, you have to visit places where the magic is still strong enough to get you there, mostly in Ireland and Germany. There is one such place deep in the Amazon, and some in Asia. We can communicate, but it requires more mana and time than we have to do regularly."

"Queens," Devon says. "We have Queens?"

"Titania is our Summer Queen," Eldan says, flicking a lock of his hair back. "She rules over life and light. Her wife is Mab, the Queen of Winter, who rules over death and darkness. The Faerie Queens."

"And they have a Court."

"Oh yes," Eldan says, taking Devon's hand and playing with it idly. He spreads Devon's fingers apart, puts them back together, strokes them and bends them absently. "The Lords and Ladies of the Court."

That's impressive. "So why aren't all of you there?"

"Banishment, or we weren't important enough to be welcomed at Court," Eldan says. "I banished myself. I didn't agree with the Queens' policy of live and let die."

"You mean live and let live."

"No," Eldan says. "Look, this isn't a palace. We scrape by. But this city doesn't have much in the way of magic, especially with the humans clearing every bit of land they can get their hands on. And I chose to be in the city because our kind needs to adapt, or we're going to become extinct. This is an experiment, as far as the Queens are concerned, and if we fail, they'll write us off. We don't have support. If we fail, the Fae stay withdrawn in their forests until there aren't any left. And that will happen. I'm doing what I have to in order to survive.

"The people here are my friends," Eldan continues. "They're here because they believe in what I want to do, and because they're loyal to me, and some of them, because they have nowhere else to go. It's live or let *die*, Devon, because dying is all we'll do in the end."

Devon sits silent. He looks around at the décor: brick walls, abstract art, metal and wood and cushions and colorful rugs. It's only a matter of time before it's gone. Eldan's doing admirable things, if he's telling it as it is. But, still, why should Devon jump on a sinking ship?

"Maybe because things move slower than you might think," Eldan says. "And while you are here, you'll have a place to belong, perhaps? We have a place for you, Devon. We want you here."

"What can I do?" Devon says, throwing up his hands. "I'm not a dancer. I don't do burlesque. I don't bartend. I can't be a bouncer. I can't cook. So what do I do here?"

"Whatever you like," Eldan says, smiling. Devon's stomach drops just a little at how pretty he is. "We can teach you any trade you want to learn. You can keep your human jobs if you like, and pay a little rent. We *do* need money here, after all. You can contribute in any way that pleases you. We don't want to force you to do anything."

"What about my old life?" Devon asks. "What if I'm not ready to give it up?"

"Then don't," Eldan says with a shrug. "Like I said, we don't want to force you into anything. We just want to help you."

"No strings?"

"Oh yes, strings," Eldan says, smiling mischievously. "We want you to be a part of our world as much as we would be a part of yours. Like I said, we ask that you contribute. But we get the pleasure of your company and one more man in our ranks. We need that."

"Why don't you invite everyone who comes in?" Devon asks. "You have plenty of patrons."

"Oh, our patrons know that there is an open door policy. They simply prefer to make it on their own. And you're free to do that as well. We'd love for you to come any time that suits you, even if you don't take our offer to become a full-time member of our little society.

"But I will admit, I think you're special, Devon. With powers like yours, and how lost you were coming in, I think we need each other. You could help us just as much as we could help you."

Eldan is listening to his thoughts. But he doesn't bring up the thought that is coalescing in his mind. He's letting Devon do it.

"And your personal interest in me?" Devon asks. "Is that a part of it?"

"I will admit I do have a personal interest," Eldan says. "I make no secret of that. But you've already declined, and I have no plans to pursue you if you don't want me to. And you've made it abundantly clear that you don't."

"And downstairs?" Devon points out. "What was that?"

"Only a tease," Eldan says, hands up. "All in the name of training, I promise. We needed a way to get you to shield as fast as possible, and embarrassment works rather well as a motivator."

"Don't lie," Devon says, glancing up at Eldan. "You liked it."

"I wouldn't be the only one lying if I said I didn't like it," Eldan says.

"And what is that supposed to mean?"

"I can read your mind, Devon. At all times. Don't you think that means something?"

"You're the leader here; you're obviously important," Devon says. He suspects Eldan hasn't told him everything about himself, because pieces are missing—'I banished myself'? That's a story worth telling. But Devon won't push too hard, lest Eldan push back. So he adds, "I'm guessing you're more powerful."

"Mmm. Not how it works, quite. You remember my powers lie in atomic structure. My mental powers are as average as the rest of us around here, except you, of course."

"No one else plays with mind stuff?"

"Maia does, of course," Eldan says. "Being a succubus. But not like you."

Devon digests that. "So I am special."

"Yes. It would seem so."

Devon sighs and pulls his hand back from Eldan's. "And, and I'm welcome here any time?"

"Any time," Eldan says.

Devon stands. "Then I'll decline for now." He glances down at Eldan, whose face remains still and straight. "I'm not ready to give up what I have."

He lets Eldan see it in his mind. He's worked hard, fucking *hard*, for what he has. He left his family. He left what he knew and he tried to make it on his own. He hasn't failed. He still makes it; he's still his own person. And Céilí is too good to be true. It's the solution to every problem Devon has dealt with lately, and it's simply too easy. Devon doesn't believe in the easy way out. It would seem like giving up.

And besides, these people are still strangers. He thinks Eldan has been mostly honest with him, but he has no way to know for sure but to stick around and see. And he does admire what Eldan is doing. Helping him is tempting. It's just not the right time.

He'll work his way in. He'll earn it.

"Perfectly understandable," Eldan says. "And I will do my best to keep a shield around you at all times. I wish you to have privacy as well. I apologize for not doing so, up to now. It was easier, I admit. But you deserve your own safe place in your mind."

"Then teach me to shield," Devon says. "Teach me to shield well enough that even you can't hear me."

Eldan seems hesitant, and Devon wishes he could read Eldan's mind. What on earth is he worried about? Does he like having access to Devon's brain? What other hesitation could there be?

"I will do my best to teach you," Eldan says. "I need you to trust me, though. Trust that I will strengthen you as far as I can. But even that might not be enough."

Devon is suspicious. It's in his nature; he just doesn't trust that easily. How can he, when he's had no one to trust except his parents, and look what they did with it.

"Why should I trust you?" Devon asks. "I barely know you."

"Would you like to know me?" Eldan asks. "That's something you'll have to do over time. I won't sit here and tell you my life story and all my deepest secrets and innermost thoughts. That would be ridiculous; I barely know you as well."

"So we're at an impasse. I can't trust you. You can't trust me. Where does that leave us?"

"With time," Eldan says. "While we train, we get to know one another. And you get to know this whole new world, all these new people. How does that sound?"

"We'll see," Devon says. That's as generous as he can be. "I need to get going. But, thanks."

"Of course. I'll show you out."

MATES. IT'S SUCH A LOVELY concept. Some believe that mates are destined to meet and be with each other. Others think mates are chosen. Eldan takes a middle stance: Some people are simply compatible on a higher level, and why not take advantage of that by spending their lives together? People would be more fulfilled and happier if they didn't resist the connections they make, if they learned to work with each other and let love speak for itself. Of course, it's never that simple, but Eldan is a romantic at heart—why can't it work that way?

Well. Any of the seven sins, of course. But Eldan is willing to try to put aside any of his own pride, lust and gluttony in order to be what a mate might want. His mate may be Devon, maybe not. Eldan's instinct is to act on any connection in hopes of finding his mate, and he's been free with his grounded affections. He never considered that that might make him less appealing to a potential mate. Fae are not ashamed of sex as humans are. But what if his mate is a changeling like Devon? Or even a human, like Kelsi's mate? What if his future mate turns him down because they don't think him capable of monogamy?

Eldan originally hoped that Devon might be his long-sought-after mate. Their connection was instant and strong, until their differences ruined it. And now, with Devon back in Eldan's life and likely to stay, the connection is back, at least a little bit. They communicate easily. Eldan is naturally comfortable around Devon, even when he keeps his distance, and oh, the distance he keeps. And Eldan being able to hear behind Devon's shields, that has to be for a reason.

But now he has his doubts. It should be easier with a mate, and Eldan struggles with Devon. He's so angry, so distant.

Mate or not, though, Eldan so desires to know more of Devon. To see more of him. They do indeed have a connection. He felt it, Devon felt it and Eldan continues to read his mind even when others can't. That's a sign of something; it has nothing to do with Eldan's power. His own mental capabilities are average at best. He'd love to pretend he's an infallible wizard, but the truth remains: His talents lie in other areas. But his mind and Devon's mind are connected somehow. And oh, how Eldan would love to explore that more.

He has the opportunity, of course. Training. Perhaps Devon can even enter Eldan's mind with ease. There's no telling until they try. So Eldan plots as he shows Devon out; even then, yes. He plans.

"You have a look on your face," Kelsi says to him when she catches sight of him, after Devon has left. "I don't like it."

"Beautiful drow," Eldan says, feigning formality and bowing to her, referencing modern dark-skinned elf mythos. "Warrior queen. I would not dare to arrange my features in a matter that offends you."

"Oh cut it out with the *drow* thing," she says, slapping his arm. It hurts. She's even stronger than she looks. "Just say elf, you nerd. What happened up there?"

"You're the one who styled your hair like that," Eldan says, noting her dark skin and white hair. "Anyway, we talked. He declined to join us here permanently, but I believe that's only for now. His life outside of here drains him; I can see it."

"You barely know him," Kelsi reminds him. "How would you know?"

"I'm not sure, but—" Eldan pauses. *Should I speak?*

"Tell me," Kelsi says, and Eldan sighs. There's no keeping it from her, no keeping this locked away in his heart. He needs at least one confidante; that is only natural, and he is not taciturn by nature.

"I don't know, Kelsi," Eldan says. "I thought maybe Devon could be my mate, but our connection is tenuous at best. I think I may long for a mate more than my reason can compass."

"Oh, Eldan." Kelsi strokes his arm. "You won't be alone forever."

"Perhaps. But come, let's talk in private."

Eldan draws her behind his curtain before waving his hand over it, slowing and condensing the molecules until it's hard as rock.

"I can read his mind," Eldan says to her, once they're alone. "When the rest of you can't, I still can."

"That's, that's unusual," Kelsi says diplomatically. "But look, you know I've found my own mate recently—"

"Yes, indeed," Eldan says, feeling happy for her even in the midst of his own predicament. "And we will talk about that later."

"Fine, fine. But I know what it feels like, don't I? So describe it to me. How does it *feel*?"

Eldan thinks. He wants to answer her well, wants her corroboration.

What was it like? Seeing him for the first time. He was beautiful. Eldan thought everything else became lesser, somehow, as if Devon was in relief while the world went flat. He felt a sizzle, a chemistry, an *electricity* between them when they looked at each other, when they touched. Eldan had never wanted anyone as much. And that feeling has only grown since: since seeing Devon, since knowing him a little more, since feeling him and seeing even the bad in him.

"It's like he's in color and the world is grey," Eldan finally says. "Call me a silly romantic, but he stands out to me."

"Well, he doesn't stand out for me," Kelsi says. "Although I'm sure he's wonderful. And that's pretty much how I felt about Olivia."

"The mystery woman has a name!" Eldan crows. "Victory is mine."

Kelsi laughs. "Fine. Her name is Olivia Perez. I haven't introduced her to my life yet, but I want to."

"Well, we have to plan that, then," Eldan says. "Just as soon as I figure out what my intentions are with our new friend, if I have any at all."

"Your priorities are in line," Kelsi laughs. But then she sobers. "You deserve it, Eldan, if this is it. You've looked a long time."

"I don't know why I want to try. He won't have me."

Kelsi takes his hand. "He'll come around. Old man."

Eldan gasps. "I am a spry young thing!"

She hip checks him gently. "Not in your twenties, though."

"I suppose the age difference is something to consider." Eldan sighs. "I can't resist his youth. Ah, he makes me feel young again."

Kelsi laughs again. "So you don't need your many lovers now? Wasn't that their job?"

"I protest," Eldan says. "In any case, I think I'll forgo lovers until I find my mate. Maybe Devon isn't the only one who finds my former amorous actions distasteful."

Kelsi shrugs. "No harm in sex. But I guess I see what you mean."

"I suppose it sends the right message, anyway, if I'm available to whomever my soulmate should be and whenever they should appear."

"Message, huh? Which is?"

"Take me, baby?"

"Yes, I'm sure that will go over well."

"We'll see, someday." Eldan sighs, but then he glances sidelong at Kelsi. "Devon is coming back, though, did you know?"

Kelsi grins. "Good."

"Yes," Eldan says. "Good indeed."

IT TAKES A WEEK FOR Devon to return. He walks in one night with his shirt rumpled and weariness in his stance. Eldan's eyes go right to him; he's sitting among his patrons, trying to find the cause of the recent unrest, but all he's managed to learn has come from Gongor, the gruff old dwarf who comes in on weekends. And all he managed to say was, "Something's coming." No one knows what, or why, but Eldan trusts their instincts. Fae are tied to the land, and the land speaks.

"You look like you could use a drink," he says, and Devon offers him a small smile.

"I probably could," he says. "But I'll pass."

"Nonsense," Eldan says, waving at Brandon at the bar. "On the house. Whatever you like."

Brandon idles over. "What can I getcha?"

"I'll have whatever he's having," Eldan says, nodding to Devon.

Devon sighs. "Some of that cider would be nice."

"Two coming up," Brandon says, heading back to the bar.

Eldan waves to a chair at the closest table. "Grab a seat. Talk with me. We haven't seen you."

"There's a reason," Devon says, grabbing the chair and pulling it over. He plants it next to Eldan, facing him. He plops down. "Work has been offering me overtime. I had to take it."

"I hope you aren't in any trouble," Eldan says carefully. Devon just shrugs.

"No, but I could use the money," he says, frank and careless. "Why not, right?"

"Of course," Eldan says. "And what do you do, exactly?"

"I wait tables at a bar and I drive a forklift at the local supermarket. The forklift job was the one offering overtime. Someone quit, and they don't have anyone else at the moment, so I've been going in on the night shift as well as the morning."

"I was a waiter when I first arrived in Los Angeles, about, oh, forty years ago. I had a head for the business and the old drag queen who ran the bar took me under her wing and showed me the ropes. Five years later, I opened Céilí."

"I can't imagine you as a waiter." Devon looks Eldan up and down.

"Because of my outfit?" He's wearing silver pants and a tight black shirt.

"No," Devon laughs. "Just—you. You're so poised and, and elegant."

Eldan smiles sincerely. "Well, thank you."

Devon returns the smile. Then he shrugs and his face turns down. The shadows under his eyes deepen.

"You seem tired," Eldan says, as Brandon leaves the drinks. Eldan takes a small sip. "Go ahead, drink up. By all means, relax while you're here."

"Thanks."

They drink in silence, watching the dancers perform a short number on the stage. After a few minutes, Eldan flicks his eyes to Devon.

"You're a musician, I believe?"

"Yeah, I try. No one's biting, though."

"You know we have this stage, here."

Devon shakes his head. "I don't want a handout."

"So audition," Eldan says, shrugging. They already juggle Maia, Serena, Brandon, the sprites and occasionally Ruad, the cook, as well as karaoke night. With three sets a night among the five of them, one more will even out the numbers and make a complete, fair rota. "I happen to be the proprietor; I can set that up."

Devon pulls in on himself, and Eldan stops shielding for a moment to check, but Devon is remarkable. He's shielding himself.

He says, "Still feels like a handout. You've got performers already. I don't need your charity."

"We do look for new performers," Eldan says. "Acts can get stale. Adding a new slot to our rota might liven things, especially with your abilities."

"What about my abilities?"

Eldan blinks. "Well, perhaps we could train you to project into your music."

"I don't want to put thoughts into people's heads with my songs," Devon says. "That's not the point."

"Not anything suggestive. You aren't going to force anyone to like your music if it's bad. Simply supplement it with some emotion. Let them really *feel* your songs."

Devon considers, sipping his cider and eyeing Eldan warily. "That's something I could do?"

Eldan shrugs. "Why not? We can always try."

Devon nods. "Well. Let's try it. But I'm still going to audition, and I don't want you to give me a slot just because you want me here, okay? I need to really earn it."

"Of course. I would never—"

"So make it a vote. Let everyone decide, not just you. I don't trust you."

Eldan puts a hand on his chest and gasps. "Me? For shame, I have been nothing but trustworthy."

"Oh really?" Devon says. "How about spiking my coffee."

Eldan pauses. "Well. There's that."

"Ha."

"Oh, please."

Devon grins. It's a beautiful grin. His eyes scrunch up at the corners, almost closing, and all his teeth show. He has a dimple on one side, amidst his half-grown scruff, and Eldan adores everything about this man as he discovers it.

Devon clearly doesn't adore anything in return. Yet he's here.

"You know, I wonder. You don't trust us. You don't need us. You don't seem to want us. So, why are you here?"

Devon's smile fades and he stares at Eldan. "Who said I didn't want to be here?"

Eldan shrugs. "It's the impression I get."

Devon shifts. "Look, I am hesitant. Not reluctant. But I've had a lot of time to think this past week."

"Your absence isn't only for work, then."

"Of course not," Devon says.

"And?"

"I'll let you know when I figure it out myself," Devon hedges. "For now, though, I'm here for a reason."

"Ah. Yes. And what is that?"

Devon gives Eldan an unimpressed look. "Training."

"Of course. How silly of me."

Devon continues to give him the *look*. Eldan can't help but smile.

"Fine," Devon says finally. "So. Teach me."

"Very well," Eldan says. "Then stop imbibing, if you will. Don't want to skew our results."

Devon hands over his cider, and Eldan sets it on the table. He puts his own down as well.

"Okay. Now." Eldan turns to Devon and smiles. "Drop your shields. I have to check."

Devon struggles, but then his thoughts are clear to Eldan. He nods and then shields himself.

"Shield yourself again. You've had enough mana to affect you. We'll have to wait a little while for it to calm down."

"What are we going to be doing?" Devon asks, settling back with a sour look.

"First of all, we need to teach you to access your own energy so you can control your powers even when not ingesting alcohol," Eldan says. "It's essential you learn this if you want to have any control whatsoever. On the positive side, holding a mental shield requires some access to your own energy, so you're doing it instinctively on a small scale. We just need to increase that scale."

"So what am I going to have to do?"

"Oh, a bit of meditation, some visualization, a little this, a little that. You know."

"No, I don't know."

"Well, *I* know, and that's what matters, since I'm the one teaching you," Eldan says. "Now. Sit back and enjoy the show while you sober up, you lush."

DEVON IS COMPLETELY SOBER AFTER one performance—an energetic, bubbly pop song medley sung by Serena.

"She's good, isn't she?" Eldan asks.

Devon smiles. Eldan's been great: friendly, but not pushing for anything more. That lets Devon warm up a little bit, trust a little bit.

"She's great," Devon says. "I wonder why she's not signed anywhere."

"She's got no ambitions," Eldan says. "Serena is happy to sing here for the rest of us, but her true passion lies with Earth magic, which she uses distilling our liquors. She sells potions on the side, too. She's got a webpage."

Devon laughs. Actual magic potions, being sold on the Internet? The world is a strange place. "I'll have to check that out."

The medley ends, and Serena gives a little curtsy to the applause. Devon joins in, whistling for her, and Eldan directs a little clap at Devon.

"So what now?" Devon asks, when the applause dies down.

Eldan smiles at him, long and slow. "Well. Let's go over what you've done already, hmm?"

"I've made people give me tips," Devon starts, and Eldan clucks his tongue.

"Humans," he says. "So easily manipulated. We'll go over subtle suggestions again. What else?"

"I've shielded," Devon says, vividly remembering how that particular lesson went: the feel of Eldan's hands on his chest, the warmth of his whisper in Devon's ear.

"Ah, yes, you have. How about we work on that tonight? Make that as strong as it can be? Then we can work on going into others' minds while you're shielded, let you multitask a little bit, yes?"

"Sounds good to me," Devon says. "So what do I do?"

Eldan faces Devon. "I want you to shield. Concentrate very hard on it."

"Okay."

Devon closes his eyes, and imagines the shield: his impenetrable bubble of electrified titanium. Or whatever really strong metal conducts electricity. Uranium? *No, concentrate.* A metal bubble around his brain, completely impervious, electrically charged, and—

Bzz. It's a little zap, warm and fuzzy. Devon blinks his eyes open; Eldan is smirking at him in a worrying fashion.

Bzz. "What are you doing?" he asks.

Bzz. Eldan's smirk grows. "Testing you."

"Knock it off," Devon says. *Bzz.* The zaps are not exactly unpleasant, but they aren't very comfortable. They have a sense of *wrongness.* They're intrusive.

"No," Eldan says happily. *Bzz,* harder this time, more of a shock. Devon winces.

"Hey, stop it," Devon says, nervous laughter edging his voice.

"No," Eldan says again. *Bzz,* even harder. "Shield me."

"You're distracting me," Devon says, closing his eyes.

"Yes, I am," Eldan says. *Bzz.* "How would you like some dinner, by the way? I'm sure we could get something from the kitchen if you like."

Bzz. "No, thanks." *Shield, shield. Bzz.*

"Concentrate, Devon," Eldan chides. "I may not be getting through, but I am weakening you. Don't let me." *Bzz.*

Devon holds firm, re-fortifying himself. This is the work of his mind. As long as he can still think, he can think himself a shield. He doesn't get tired of thinking, it just *is.*

Oh! The shield just has to *be.*

Devon sighs and opens his eyes. "I'd love some dinner, thanks," he says, knowing without a doubt that his shield will hold as long as he thinks it will. *That's the secret; it has to be.* "What's on the menu?"

"We'll be out of the salmon by this time, but there's stew," Eldan says. The next buzz is barely discernible, and Devon can't help but smile. *Yes.*

And then—

BZZ.

"Ow!" Devon cries, reaching up for his head. That one *hurt*, as if someone banged on the metal bubble with a jackhammer. It *vibrated* and it was *wrong* and *fuck.*

"You're not quite a master yet, Devon. Don't get cocky," Eldan says. "But you are doing very well. You need practice before those knocks on your mind don't bother you."

Devon rubs his temple. "Will they ever go completely away?"

"Oh no. And you wouldn't want them to. They'll warn you when someone is trying to intrude on your thoughts, and you *want* to be sensitive to them."

That makes sense. "Okay then. But don't do that again, that last one."

"Oh, I will, though," Eldan says. "And you'll ask me to do it, one day. You'll need to be tested as you get stronger and learn how to control your powers."

"How will I get stronger? Is it like working out a muscle?"

Eldan tilts his head. "Maybe. You do have to practice to strengthen it. But it also has to do with partaking of mana and learning to channel your natural stores. It's like learning to swim, really. You've got the instinct to keep afloat, but you have to learn how to access that instinct so you don't panic and drown. And eventually you will become a wonderful swimmer; you'll learn how to hold your breath and how to keep water out of your nose. You'll learn different strokes and how to stay afloat even when you're tired. You're surrounded by a world that could kill you, but you have it in you to master it. You just have to learn. Does that make sense?"

"I guess," Devon says. "And you're my swim instructor?"

"Yes, that's how it seems." Eldan smiles and tosses his head back. "Aren't you lucky?"

Devon laughs, and Eldan joins him. His laugh is high and pretty, like the rest of him.

"You did well," Eldan says. "Really. I was hard on you, and your shields still held."

"It felt like you were gonna pierce my brain there for a minute," Devon says, unable to keep a little accusation out of his tone.

Eldan smiles and shrugs, unapologetic. "You should be prepared for much worse. I won't go any easier on you."

"Well, at least you're honest about it," Devon half-grumbles, and Eldan grins at him.

"Come on, let's get some drinks!" Eldan says, raising his voice. He stands, offering a hand to Devon. "Let's go join the crew."

Devon regards his pale, slender hand for a moment before he slides his own into it. "All right."

Eldan pulls him up and tugs him along, winding between tables until they reach the front corner, where Eldan's crew is seated. Maia, Serena and Kelsi are at the table. Brandon comes out from behind the bar with a tray of bottled drinks and hands them out at the table. Devon sips carefully. It's a very sweet drink, tasting of honey with a floral accent. It has to be mead.

"Let's all salute our newest friend here," Eldan calls, "who just got a proverbial hit over the head and managed to stand up beneath it beautifully! To Devon!"

"Devon!" everyone calls, and Devon can't help but grin. *It feels nice to be appreciated and welcomed.*

Eldan throws a friendly, casual arm around his shoulders. "So how about some stew and good conversation?" He grins. "I can guarantee the stew, but you'll have to forgive me, I don't know where to find the latter."

Kelsi pokes Eldan in the arm. He winces and says *ow*, then juts his lower lip in a pout.

"That hurt," he says petulantly, and Kelsi pouts right back at him. He rolls his eyes and then glances over to Devon.

"I need you to nurse my wounds," he says, completely deadpan, and Devon can't help it, he snorts. Eldan immediately smiles as if the sun came out and dried up all his sorrows.

"I think your wounds are fine," Devon says, and Eldan sighs dramatically.

"No one understands my struggles," he says. Across the table, Maia rolls her eyes.

"Just go get one of the sprites to nurse your wounds," she says.

Devon shifts, but Eldan remains half-draped over him.

"I do not partake of wound-nursing of that sort anymore, thank you very much," Eldan says. Before Devon can even blink, he continues, "Now who's going to go get Devon some stew from the kitchen? I'm not it."

Brandon sighs and raises his hand. "Be right back."

And then Devon is leaning back and drinking, and he feels at home. Easy. Among friends. It's not something he's familiar with. His family gatherings were always small, because his parents left Ireland and their families along with it. And he never really had close friends, not close enough to party with.

This is the first time Devon's felt like part of a group.

It feels pretty good.

"Sing!" Serena says, pointing at him. "You're a singer aren't you? You should sing!"

Devon protests, but everyone joins in. "Sing! Sing!"

"Okay," he says. "I'll audition for you," he adds, with a look at Eldan, who claps and nods.

He hops up on the low stage. "Uh, guitar?"

"Backstage," Eldan calls, and Devon turns. There's a door off to the side, and he jogs over and opens the door. Inside the backstage area is a guitar on a stand in the back corner. He grabs it and makes his way back to the stage.

He pulls up a stool from the back of the stage, sits and adjusts the microphone. "Hi. I'm Devon. I'm gonna sing for you."

There are cheers, and he strums a few random chords. Now what song to pick? Something easy, or something to impress? Something familiar to the crowd, or something to spice things up? Or... well. Why not show his own music a little? He strums, singing

> *There's a piece of me that finds*
> *Your eyes across the room every time*
> *Can I listen, or am I reaching*
> *To the little voice inside my head preaching*

Devon continues to the final chorus.

I'd give the clothes on my back
I'd give the very last cent
I'd give my whole heart into your hands
Just tell me if it's just me
Tell me where our story lands

He strums a finish, and the room erupts in cheers. He laughs, sets the guitar against the stool, waves and nods his way off the stage and back to his seat. He takes a big swig of his mead and accepts the laughter and the praise from the table.

"So," Eldan says into his ear as he sits, with the adrenaline of performance still in his blood. "What do you think? Will you stay?"

It's tempting. It's very, very tempting. But he still has a life outside of this place, and he's not ready to leave everything behind. He still wants his jobs; he still wants to try the music business. He hasn't let go of that. But it's nice here; it's more than nice here. He could get used to it.

"Not yet," he says. "But I'll keep it in mind."

Eldan smiles. "We're always here for you if you change your mind."

He knows. And it's good.

DEVON ALMOST CHANGES HIS MIND often over the next couple of weeks. Céilí is more like a home than his apartment some days, as if he belongs there, and leaving gets hard. Nights they get him up on stage are the best, because he really reaches people when he sings. They enjoy him, and he doesn't have to be magical or anything else, he just has to be.

He really fits in. He makes friends with almost everyone. Serena is kind and happy, as if she's always bubbling joy, like champagne. Brandon is wry and sly and a good friend who always has an ear available. Kelsi is sweet and surprisingly fun. Even Maia is okay, sometimes. Only the dancers—the sprites, people call them—are distant. He doesn't even know their names. But he gets acquainted with several regular customers.

And Eldan. Eldan is many things. He's smart and straightforward, but silly and strange. Devon likes his little bit of mystery. He's under the impression that he's just scratched the surface with Eldan. There's more to discover as they become friends. And god, he's nice to look at, too.

One night, a week into his training, Devon finds himself coming off stage on a high.

"Have a drink!" someone calls—a female voice, probably Serena—and Devon nods. Within moments a drink is shoved in his hand, and he drinks it down. He's sampled most of the menu by now, with Serena and Brandon's encouragement, and the drinks are all good, unusual, but good. The cider remains his favorite, though, so when he finishes the fruity whatever he'd been handed, he heads to the bar and asks for a cider.

"Not a chance," Brandon says. "I'm gonna close up soon, and then we're doing shots."

"We as in you and me?"

"We as in *everybody*. It's been too long since we all partied together and it's time."

"Okay," Devon says. "Can I have a cider anyway?"

Brandon laughs. "Fine. Here you go."

Devon takes it and heads back to the front table, sliding into what is now his seat. Across the table, Maia raises an eyebrow, but says nothing. Devon shakes his head and takes a sip of his cider. He and Maia don't seem to click, which is not a big deal, in the grand scheme of things. Devon just doesn't get good feelings around her and he trusts his instincts.

"Ready for a party?" Eldan asks, leaning on the chair next to Devon.

"Sure," Devon says. "I haven't been to one in a while. Not since, I don't know, like six months ago? I got invited to one by the girls at work."

"How was it?"

"There were way too many girls," Devon says. "I think they wanted me to be their 'gay friend' or something. I don't know, I never asked."

"Why didn't you go out with them again?"

"I guess I wasn't a lot of fun," Devon says. "I didn't mesh well with the group. We didn't have anything to offer each other, so I turned down the half-assed second invite and haven't been asked since."

Eldan tilts his head and frowns. "Have you always been so lonely?"

That stings because Devon knows it's true. But he doesn't feel like talking about it much, so he just shrugs. "I guess."

Eldan puts a hand on his shoulder. "No more," he says. "You're here now. As much or as little as you want to be."

Devon nods, not sure how to respond, and Brandon wanders over with a tray of shots.

"Here we go," he says. "Everybody up; we don't sit on our asses for shots."

"Get some music going," Serena calls out. As Devon stands, one of the dancers heads backstage, and a few seconds later music pours out of the speakers: a dance beat with a high voice, something Devon vaguely recognizes from the bar where he works.

"Everybody take a shot!" Brandon calls, and Devon takes a shot glass along with everybody else. "One, two, three!"

The liquor burns its way down his throat, and he shakes his head to clear it. The shot glass goes rim down on the table, and then Brandon waves his hand in a circle, the sign for *go again*.

Devon takes another shot glass, and Brandon cheers. "Yes, more, more!"

It takes three more shots before Brandon is satisfied with everyone's level of drunkenness, or at least with Devon's, because it's Devon he pulls up on stage to dance with. Several of the others are already dancing, including Kelsi, whom Devon bumps into several times. It's not a big stage, and they're all in a tight group.

And then Eldan appears. He took shots, but at some point he slipped away from the table, and Devon lost track of him. But now he's dancing with Kelsi, body long and sensual as it twists and turns. And then it's twisting and turning with Devon, somehow slipping into Devon as he turns away from Brandon, and then Brandon and Kelsi dance, and it's just them. Eldan smells amazing, like *man*, clean and almost minty, and he dances close to Devon, closer than Brandon did, *too* close, but Devon loves it. It's been a long time since he danced with an attractive man, and he's always found dancing fun in and of itself. He rests his hands on Eldan's waist, and Eldan laughs and raises his arms and he's beautiful. *So* beautiful. Why didn't Devon want to be with him?

Oh yeah. The fact that Eldan had sex with two people and then propositioned Devon not twenty minutes later. He's promiscuous. For some people, sex is just sex, and they're welcome to it as long as they don't hurt anybody. But Devon is hurt when he's shared with others. He's a jealous man, deep down, because when a lover doesn't focus solely on him, he feels neglected. He doesn't want to be one of many; he wants to be *one*. He wants to be special and adored, not a pastime. Eldan—Eldan has pastimes.

That's why Devon can't act on his attraction to Eldan, no matter how strong it grows. He can't put himself in a position to be hurt. He gets hurt often enough without his own help.

But right now there's drink, and there's dancing, and Eldan is here, and he's not hitting on Devon, he's just dancing. They're friends; they can be friends. And Devon is so wanted here, and so, so *comfortable*, and he has a room upstairs he hasn't been to since it was shown to him, and he has all these friends now. So Devon loses track of things after a while. They do more shots, and he sips one cider, and then another, and Eldan stays by his side and dances with him and laughs with him and takes sips of his drink. At one point, Devon leans into him and sighs, tired and feeling a little lost, and Eldan kisses his sweaty temple. And then Devon finds himself holding Eldan's hand as Eldan guides him up the stairs.

"Where are we going?" he hears himself asking.

"You're going to sleep," Eldan says, pulling him gently down the hall to the last door on the left. "You can't go home like this, so I'm taking you to your rooms."

"I like that they're mine," Devon mumbles, running a hand down the door jamb. "It feels safer."

"Safer than what, honey?" Eldan asks softly, shunting him in through the door.

"Like, safer than if I didn't have a room here," Devon says. He sits on the bed, and then wobbles; wow, he is very drunk. His head swims. "You can't disappear if I have a room here."

Eldan makes a soft noise, like a coo, and then he gently presses Devon down onto his side. "Lie down, okay?"

"I don't want you to disappear," Devon says, drunkenly honest. "I like this place. Even though I like my old life too. The new one can stay. Why can't I have both?"

"You can have both," Eldan says. "You're doing it right now."

"Not forever though. I don't wanna do it forever."

"Whatever you want is okay, sweetie," Eldan says, and Devon notices he's talking to him like a child.

"Not a kid," Devon protests, and Eldan chuckles softly.

"No, you're not." He pulls a blanket over Devon's body, and Devon hugs the pillow under his head. "But you are very drunk. So get some sleep."

"'Kay."

Devon lets himself relax, boneless, into the bed. Curling up is nice, and his shoes are gone, and he's heavy and the bed sinks with him.

He drifts, and, before he knows it, the sun is peeking into the room and piercing his eyes even behind his eyelids, and he wakes from a deep sleep.

He's definitely hungover, but when he heads downstairs, everyone else is, too. They're all nursing coffees and eating toast and they welcome him with groaned hellos and not much else. But he feels the camaraderie. They all got drunk together; they're all paying for it together. Even Eldan is out of sorts, but he smiles at Devon as he sits in his chair and joins them.

Devon might be able to get used to this.

THREE WEEKS INTO HIS TRAINING, Devon loses his bar job.

"We have too many employees," his boss says. "You're a good worker, but you're the least senior. We have to let you go."

And there's nothing Devon can do about it. It's not about him; it's cutbacks, and he'll have to do without. On the one hand, that's money lost, money he can't afford to lose. He's got bills like everybody else; he has to pay for things. He didn't make a ton of bank on that job, but his tips were good and it gave him some wiggle room to cover what his supermarket job didn't.

On the other hand, more time at Céilí.

When Devon takes note of that positive, he realizes that it *is* a positive to him. He likes spending time there. It's not only about him reconnecting with his origins; it's not just curiosity about a magical world; it's not a passing thing for him. He enjoys going there and he enjoys his training and spending time with Eldan. He likes that damn bar and the performances and the food, and he likes the feel of the bed in the apartment set aside for him. He likes that it *is* set aside for him.

He likes that Céilí is *there*. He likes that he belongs there, that they welcome him. And that's the basis of its appeal: He is truly welcomed there.

He knows there's distance between him and the rest of the world.

But not at Céilí. He's right in the center of it, and he's welcome. He's not strange there; he's not just put up with. They *want* him there. Every time he walks in he is greeted by whomever happens to be there. And Eldan, who is always on hand whenever Devon happens by.

And that's a relationship to think about. Eldan has been nothing but helpful and friendly to Devon, and Devon has found himself warming to him. They're getting to know each other through the training. Eldan has so much humor: He's melodramatic for the fun of it; he likes words and the whimsy they can bring. He's supportive and he believes in Devon. And Devon likes his company and more and more finds himself respecting Eldan as the leader he really is. He's a fantastic, attentive teacher, but he's also a good friend to everyone, while remaining as authoritative as needs be.

Devon isn't immune to guilt for having judged him so harshly for so long. But then, there's nothing he can do now but be as friendly as he can in return. *That's what friends do, right? They act friendly.*

He's still pretty new at this.

IT TURNS OUT FRIENDS DO more than act friendly.

"Why so down?" Eldan asks, the evening of the day after Devon lost the bar job. "You're usually so *cheerful.*"

"Ha ha," Devon says, half-smiling. "Before you tease me anymore, you should know I am actually in trouble. I lost one of my jobs."

Eldan nods. Devon blinks at him, having expected some form of sympathy. Instead, he just stares at Devon.

"What?" Devon asks.

Eldan sighs. "You haven't found the irony. If it even is irony, so hard to tell."

"What irony?"

Eldan taps on Devon's head. "Remember how I own a bar?"

Devon shakes his head. "I'm not asking you for a job. And you haven't had time for the rota, I remember that much—"

"No, you aren't on the rota yet, but you've managed to perform a few times anyway, right? And besides, you're not asking me at all. I'm hiring you. We need someone to do odd jobs, help out here and there. Every job is covered, but everyone could use a hand as well. Do you think you could float around, learn the ropes, give everyone a little boost?"

Devon instantly wants to say no, but he stops himself. *Why* does he want to say no? There's something unattractive about handouts, of course, but is there a truly good reason to say no, other than his own pride?

He has resisted the call of Céilí. And it has called; it's called to him from the moment he walked up to it. And it's only gotten stronger: the want, the need to be here. And his reasons for resistance are running out.

"Okay, fine," Devon hears himself saying. "When do I start?"

"Well, let's go over your other job schedule, and we'll pencil you in when you can make it, hmm?"

Eldan turns away, but Devon catches him with a hand on his arm. Eldan turns and quirks an eyebrow.

"I just wanted to say thanks," Devon says. "It means a lot."

"You won't be thanking me when I have you cleaning the bathrooms," Eldan says happily. "Now. Schedule?"

"I work the supermarket Friday through Wednesday, in the mornings."

"Well, then come over every day after that, around five?" Eldan says. "And you can have, oh, let's say Thursdays off, to make it even and give you a full day to yourself. And I promise we won't break your back while you're here."

Devon shrugs. "Sounds good to me."

"We can change that as you please," Eldan adds. "So you can continue your music and have a life outside these walls. We'll call it as it comes, yes?"

"Thank you," Devon says. "I mean it."

Eldan shrugs, a big, expansive gesture. "Well, we can't have you on the street, now, can we? And besides, look how easily you fit into our schedule."

Look how easy I fit in. Devon smiles. "So, anything tonight? Or are we training?"

"Mmm, both," Eldan says. "Come with me."

He leads Devon to the kitchen, where a rather large man with a beard is chopping onions. The smell is strong, and Devon unconsciously pulls his head back as they approach the table.

"My dear friend," Eldan says, sauntering up to the counter with apparently no aversion to the thick onion reek. "Ruad. Help has arrived."

The bearded man—Ruad, Devon assumes—glances up and smiles. "This how you woo a man these days, Eldan?"

Eldan throws his head back and laughs. "Think it'll work?"

"Maybe tomorrow night. I'm making salmon."

"Oooh, your salmon is delightful."

"Everything I make is," Ruad says. He glances at Devon. "You the help?"

"That's me," Devon says, putting on a smile.

"Well, you look like you could lift a broom, maybe some crates," Ruad says. "I need someone to follow me around and clean up what I leave behind, maybe do some inventory. Think you could manage?"

"I do inventory at my other job. And sweeping's easy enough."

Ruad laughs, a booming sound. "You say that now. Just wait."

He takes the onions in his huge hands and dumps them into a big pot, and Devon notices an actual, iron, round, big fucking cauldron, right there next to the industrial stove. It's on a slab of concrete with a little fire stoked right beneath it. A stew bubbles within.

"Spicing things up tonight?" Eldan asks.

"I'm caramelizing these for the brie burgers," Ruad says, stirring the onions. "Want anything special for yourself tonight?"

"I will eat one of your delicious brie burgers," Eldan says. "They sound delightful. Devon, I believe, will choose what he wants to eat when there's a break in his work, which he will get to in approximately one minute. Just need to give him some instructions. Listen in, Ruad."

He turns to Devon and smiles. "You have more work than just sweeping and cleaning up after our wonderful chef here. I also want you to try to put a thought into Ruad's head. Yes?"

"I can try," Devon says. He's been working on his energy—moving and controlling it—and he's been doing better. But he hasn't successfully pushed a thought into someone's head.

"Good. Then this is what you'll try to tell Ruad," he says, stepping in far too close and whispering in Devon's ear. He breathes, "Ask him where his club is."

Then he's gone, pulled back from Devon's space with a wink. "Have fun." He whirls away, and the kitchen doors shut behind him with a *woosh* and a *clack*.

Ruad nods at Devon and then nods at the wall. "Broom's there. Clean rags hang in front of the sink, dirty ones go in the basket underneath. Try to keep up."

ELDAN FINDS HIMSELF WITH LITTLE to do while Devon starts his work, so he takes a seat on his throne and looks out over the bar. They're not packed tonight, perhaps a smaller crowd than average, but it's a beautiful evening and Eldan's not all that surprised. Gains can be made on an evening like this—not a finer one to be found. People will be feeling expansive and going out on the town; people on whom the Fae feed in each capacity, whether that Fae is a thief or a sex worker or a hustler or a downtrodden worker like Devon. That's where they exist, most of them: on the edge of society.

Eldan wishes he could see more for his people. There's not a lot of fellow-feeling among the Fae, but Eldan has lived long enough on the edges to have developed a fellow-feeling with his magical siblings here in the badlands. And even those back home, yes, because the only difference between them is location. All of them are in danger of disappearing.

But yes, he wants more for them. Eldan does very well for himself, carving out his existence here, using his immense power for glamour tricks and business management. And leading, he supposes. These Fae look up to him still, even if his titles mean nothing out here. They look to him for an example, for authority, for sustenance and entertainment. They look to him as though he were a kindly uncle suddenly burdened with custody, and he does his best to provide for them what he can. After all, he opened up Céilí on his own, with the hope of providing a haven, and he's done his job well. These Fae have a safe place because of him, and he's proud of what he's done. It's more than the Queens have ever done. They didn't create Summerland, they just rule it. Older gods than they did that work. Eldan built Céilí from the ground up.

He knows his people. And the thing is, he's not sure he knows them *right now*. Something is off, and has been for at least a couple of months, but it's been getting worse: the unrest, the discomfort crackling in the crowd. His people are not jovial; they are not at ease as they have been. People are unsure and walking under dark clouds.

He's tried to get words on the matter, but no one can express it. It's as if the air itself is oppressive. And it's speaking to them, to all of them, Eldan included. Why should that be? Things have been going well, at least for Eldan himself. But it's as if there's a sword hanging, ready to fall, and Eldan can't see it. The hairs on the back of his neck stand up when he contemplates it, as if they're reaching out to feel the blade as it hovers, filled with so much potential energy that could, at any moment, become kinetic.

But there's nothing he can do but wait. There's no handle for him to grasp, no loose edge for him to pry. The mystery is smooth and implacable.

"Kelsi," Eldan calls, as she walks by, apparently on her way to other business.

"Yeah, boss?" she asks.

"Get whatever paperwork you haven't done and bring it to me. I'll help tonight."

"You sure?" she asks. "It's boring as hell—"

"Take the night off from being my secretary and yes-man," he replies. "I have a hankering for some drudgery to take my mind off of things."

WHAT FOLLOWS FOR DEVON IS a storm of chopped vegetables, seeds, juices, discarded bits of meat and various other food-based debris. Ruad pushes through his recipe efficiently, but he leaves behind him a mess, and it's all Devon can do to dart in and clean up when Ruad slips away to stir or flip or gather more ingredients. He's like a focused, productive tornado, order in the middle and chaos on the outside. He leaves a wake of detritus, but he also creates a meal for forty people in an hour and a half spent between his counters, the stove and his gigantic grill.

And the entire time, Devon chants in his head, *Where's your club? Where's your club?* When he has a moment to breathe, he imagines a line between them, like a telephone line, transmitting the information from his head to Ruad's head, but Ruad's doesn't look at him beyond a smile here and there when Devon cleans up after him.

"How are you doing, boy?" Ruad asks, when he has a moment to wipe his hands and his brow as the burgers grill.

"Fine," Devon says with a huff of breath. Ruad laughs boisterously.

"You're keeping up fine. Don't worry about it."

"I'm more worried about my training, to be honest," Devon admits. "I haven't gotten through to you at all."

"You've poked here and there. But you're not doing it strongly enough. You need to give it a real heave, you know? You've got to get through layers of bone and brain before you can really get to someone's mind, see? And you're getting through your own mind at the same time. How are you visualizing the transfer?"

Devon blinks. "Um. A telephone line."

"That's not going to do it," Ruad says. "You have to imagine an ice pick. A jackhammer. Something sharp and forceful. Not a telephone line, that'll get you nowhere. No one *wants* to listen. You have to *make* them listen, right?"

"I can try," Devon says.

"Well, give it a go while we've got a minute. Come on."

Devon concentrates. The energy tingles in his fingertips, and then, automatically and absolutely ridiculously, he imagines not an ice pick, but an icicle, jamming the thought, *where's your club?* right into Ruad's head. He imagines it piercing the man's brain. Ruad raises his head and a grin forms on his face.

"Hey," he says. "I think I heard that. One more time. Really give it to me!"

Devon imagines the icicle sharp and cold and jammed straight into the meat of Ruad's brain, and Ruad laughs.

"Oh, boy!" he says. "Who the hell knows where that old thing rolled off to? It's been gone too long to tell. But you tell your Eldan that you did it, kid. That was fantastic!"

"I didn't know telepathy could be so violent," Devon says. Ruad laughs again, grabs a huge platter of bun halves and lifts the lid to the grill. He starts putting burgers on the buns as he speaks.

"It is if you want people to pay attention," Ruad says. "Minds are hard to work with, remember that. They're naturally resistant to outside influence. So if you've got the power to be influential, you have to make it so they can't ignore you. Now, that won't work against someone shielding, of course, but if someone's just walking around in their everyday life, they'll hear you."

"What if I want them to think it's their own thought?"

Ruad *hmphs*. "Well. Start with too much. Then let Eldan pull you back, he's better at the subtle stuff."

At least he has progress to report to Eldan. The first in three weeks. His palms start to sweat, and he's jittery. He's anxious to go tell him, almost *excited* about it. *No, definitely excited, why deny it?* He wants to *brag* a little.

"Are we done?" Devon asks.

"I'll need you for inventory after the dinner rush is over," Ruad says. "Maybe I'll even have you help on dishes. Why don't you take a plate, go eat and come back when you're done?"

"Are you sure?" Devon asks. "I could help serve."

"Don't even try," Ruad warns. "The sprites have dibs on serving dinner, and they won't want you taking that job. We all fight to keep our places here, you see. Just do what you're told for now, and keep your head down until you find an opening."

Huh. Maybe he doesn't belong as thoroughly as he thought, but it makes sense. He's brand new, and the vets don't want him usurping them. *That's reasonable enough.*

Devon doesn't really feel so understanding when the dancing girls and boys pass by him on his way to meet Eldan. They give him a *look*, especially one of the boys who was with Eldan the first night they met.

Devon rolls his eyes and heads to Eldan's curtain, knocking on its hard surface before he realizes: *Eldan's probably back there with someone.*

He turns and starts to walk away, but on the edge of his hearing, Eldan says, "Come in!" The curtain rustles. Devon turns back and peeks in.

"Sorry to interrupt," he says, almost not wanting to look in the room.

"You interrupt nothing but paperwork," Eldan says, waving him in and putting aside a paper with lots of tiny writing on it. "A welcome interruption. How did you do with Ruad?"

"Well enough," Devon says. "I swept up after him. And he doesn't know where his club is," he adds, carefully casual.

Eldan doesn't miss that. He smirks and nods. "Leave it to Ruad," he says, somewhat mysteriously. "Congratulations on your first successful transfer of thought. However did you manage?"

"An icicle," Devon says, nodding. Eldan blinks.

"An icicle?"

"Instead of a telephone line."

Eldan frowns at him. "Hm. Not very subtle."

Devon laughs. "It was Ruad's suggestion. Well, he said ice pick; my brain kind of changed it up—"

Eldan laughs. "Of course. Silly me." He gestures to the chair next to him. "Eat with me."

Devon sits down, and Eldan waves his hand. The curtain draws aside, revealing the bar. Eldan waves his hand again, this time to one of the serving boys.

"Two of the special," Eldan says. He glances at Devon. "Unless you'd rather have stew?"

"No thanks," Devon says. "Special's fine." He turns back to Eldan. "What's with the stew, anyway? Why is it always on the menu?"

"Let's just call it Ruad's safety meal," Eldan says. "He never runs out of it."

Devon decides not to push it further. He's not in the mood for half-answers and Eldan doesn't seem forthcoming. He returns to his paperwork, and his eyes squint down at it.

"Maybe you need glasses," Devon suggests.

Eldan glances up. "I'm sorry?"

"You should get glasses," Devon says. "You're squinting at the paper."

Eldan raises an eyebrow. "I'd like to see you read this chicken scratch without squinting."

Devon holds out his hand, and Eldan deposits the little stack of papers in it. Devon stares at the writing. It's a cramped scrawl, a report on distillation.

"Serena's writing?"

"No," Eldan says with a grin. "Mine."

Devon bursts out laughing. "Well, why do you write like that, then?"

"That's how I write when I go fast," Eldan says, reading again. "Serena's going to need a lot more yeast if we're to keep up with production of our lovely mana-infused moonshine."

"How does that work?" Devon asks offhand, as one of the dancing boys arrives with their food. "Does she put her own mana into it?"

"Mmm?" Eldan blinks, accepting his plate. "Oh, no. She pulls it from the Earth. She's a pixie; as long as she is connected to the Earth, she can access its power. We're very lucky to have her for this."

"And, do the people who come here really need the alcohol?" Devon asks, taking a bite. He chews quickly and swallows. "Why consume it that way? Can't you put it in, I don't know, water?"

"Alcohol has more life in it than water, thanks to the yeast," Eldan says, talking around his food. "There's magic in all life forms, energy. Serena makes use of that. And besides, alcohol sells."

"But what does everyone get out of it?" Devon says. "I mean, if the alcohol is a depressant, and the mana is like a stimulant, right?"

Eldan smiles at him. "When do you find you need a boost of energy?"

"Early morning," Devon says.

"And when would you need a boost of energy after a long day?"

"Oh. So it's just a boost in the evening?"

Eldan shrugs. "It works. I try not to think too hard about it. I opened a bar to appeal to the communal and celebratory aspects of Fae culture. A place to relax and rest after a long day struggling through the human world, where we don't belong. So a bar it is, and putting the mana in the alcohol was simply a concession to what they would be doing already: drinking."

"Oh," Devon says. "That makes sense now."

Eldan takes a big bite of his burger and chews around stuffed cheeks. Devon laughs and then takes a bite of his own.

"Hello?"

Brandon stands before them and waves his hand back and forth.

"Yes, hi," he says, raising his eyebrows. "Been here for a moment now. Um. Eldan, phone for you."

Eldan wipes his mouth with his napkin. "Be right back, then."

Brandon goes with him, leaving Devon alone. He continues to eat. Why not—he doesn't need company.

But he's not left without company for long. Kelsi comes in, waving at him.

"Hi," she says. "You and Eldan were deep in conversation for a while there. You didn't watch the performance."

"No, sorry. Who was it?"

"Me," Kelsi says. "I play violin in my spare time. Sometimes I play it for people when Ruad doesn't take his slot." She takes Eldan's seat. "And you sing. Quite well."

"Thank you," Devon says. "I just—I don't know, I like to sing. And play."

"Well, Eldan's not the only one who wants you here," Kelsi says, smiling. She's got a really beautiful smile. "We all like you."

"Thanks?" Devon says, laughing nervously. "Um. I do like it here."

"Yeah," Kelsi says. "Look. I just need to ask you. Are you, are you interested in Eldan?"

Devon blinks. "Um?"

"I ask for a reason. I, he's into you, okay? You know that. But he's not into you the same way he's into everyone else. And I don't know if you're trying to be his friend or if you've got more in mind—"

"Look," Devon says. "I'm not trying to drag him around. I like him well enough. I just, I don't know." And he doesn't. Eldan isn't what Devon first thought; he's not a playboy with no regard for other people. He's seen that in being his friend. He doesn't always act as Devon would, but that doesn't make him a bad person. He's still Eldan: attractive, attentive, really rather sweet and supportive. He's a lot of things Devon wants. But would he ever be what Devon needs? And could Devon be what Eldan needs? "I don't know, okay?"

"I get that it's confusing," Kelsi says. "Seriously. But look, just ask Eldan about mates, okay? Sometime, sometime in the future. Ask him what they are."

"Why don't you just tell me?" Devon asks.

"Because Eldan should be the one to explain it to you," Kelsi says.

"But—"

"Excuse me, everyone, please listen up."

Devon turns; Eldan is on stage, holding a microphone. His face is grim and beautiful under the bright lights: pale and unearthly, eyes startlingly blue even at this distance. Devon immediately sits up and focuses his attention on Eldan.

Something is wrong.

"I've just had a call from our friends in Brazil," Eldan says. "Or rather, our friend. Cristiano is on his way north to us. It seems he's the only one left." A chorus of gasps and exclamations sounds in the room. "Imanja is dead; the entire haven is dead. They were discovered, and they were killed."

He allows a moment for outcry, then he holds up his hand. Everyone falls silent.

"You are welcome to stay here if you wish," Eldan says. "There will be food and shelter. But please remember that this happened half a world away. We have time. We need to stick together, and if that means you don't feel safe going home, we'll send out for sleeping bags. Our friend Kelsi will attend to all of it."

Eldan steps back from the microphone and then heads left to the backstage area Devon's never seen. Devon stands, but Kelsi grabs his arm.

"Let Eldan be alone," she says. "I know you're new here, but this is devastating news. Just, just leave him be. I have so much to deal with—"

"Do you need help?" Devon asks. "I'm here. I might as well do something."

Kelsi sighs. "You know what you could do? You could stay. Just be here? We can use all the support we can get. Do what you got hired to do, float around and see who needs help. I have to start delegating."

She hurries away, and Devon casts around, helpless. What should he do? What can he do?

Well, he can do what he's asked. He has an apartment upstairs ready and available for him; he can stay the night. He can stay. He can go back to Ruad and finish the job he was supposed to do with him, and then, and then he can stay.

And that's what he'll do.

THERE ARE MANY LORDS AND Ladies of the Fae Court from around the world. Most stay in Summerland, where geography is different and less connected, and their dominions cross over on a global scale. They stay in Court, serving the Queens in person to gain favor. Eldan used to do that, but he left, many decades ago, and found his own way.

Imanja had been on her own for over a millennium. She preferred to stay in the human world permanently, to better watch over her subjects, to give them a haven at least three times the size of the one Eldan would one day build at Céilí. Eldan knows the tales of her well; she'd been one of his examples when he decided to venture out on his own.

Now, she's gone. She and her entire haven were destroyed by humans. It's every Fae's fear, and too often their fate: to be discovered, to be eradicated, to have their homes destroyed. Their homes were taken and their natural surroundings were destroyed. That's why there are so few left, and why the ones left are in hiding—in hiding, or in Summerland, where room has never been plentiful, where some have never been welcome.

The rest are here on Earth, and now many more of them are dead.

And Eldan doesn't know what to *do*. He and Imanja were the only Court members left in the Western Hemisphere. Now he's alone, well and truly alone in a way he can't communicate to the others. He's the only authority figure left in an entire half of the world, and his haven is small. What if he's discovered as well? If one haven could be discovered, surely another could. Imanja was powerful; she ranked as a god among the humans for a very long time. Eldan is a minor in comparison. His power is nowhere near what hers was.

His hope is that it makes him less noticeable. Maybe they can stay under the radar. But then—is his power enough to maintain their spells, especially with others that might show up? Cristiano may not be the only one, though he's the only one to call ahead. Others might come to him instead of returning to Summerland or making it alone. They would need more room, more shelter, more protections.

He needs to do *something*. He can't seem to figure out *what*.

If only he had someone to *talk* to. Someone who would just *listen*, who could be there for him in the way he needs. He wants a mate more and more. He wants that connection; he wants it to be made and fulfilled. He wants Devon.

But they're still only friends, because Devon has shown no further interest. And Eldan hasn't pressed. He genuinely wants to be his friend and he will learn to be content if that's all Devon ever wants. But he aches for a mate, for someone to understand him completely, to embrace all that he is and accept it. He wants it so badly.

So why can't he have *something*?

Devon is one of them now. Eldan left him alone last night after his pronouncement. Now Eldan can call him and ask him to come by, and then he'll have someone to talk to, at least. A *friend*.

A voice in the back of his mind protests that he can always talk to Kelsi, or Maia or any one of the others. But Eldan's heart rejects it. Only Devon will do.

Eldan doesn't have much use for a cell phone, but perhaps he should invest. Perhaps they all should. Several of his little court have them, despite legends of magic destroying technology. That's not true: Technology uses energy, just as magic does, and magic can supplement technology rather nicely, and vice-versa—with *care*. And Eldan would like to experience texting. That would be convenient, and it's rather clever.

He picks up the phone in his room and dials Devon's number, which he long ago memorized.

"Hello?"

"Devon," Eldan says. "I was wondering if you were available anytime soon."

"I'm actually downstairs," Devon says, and forever wins himself a place in Eldan's heart. He's here. In the time of crisis, he's *here.*

"Good. Go to the second floor and head to the door at the opposite end of the hall. I'll meet you there."

He hangs up and practically floats through his apartment to the staircase toward the front of the building, which is the only one up to the third floor where he resides. He skips down the steps and then opens the door to the second floor as only he can. He keeps it locked at all times with his magic.

Devon appears at the end of the hall, and Eldan enjoys watching him approach, hands in his pockets, shoulders a bit hunched. His clear brown eyes seem questioning.

"What's going on? Everyone's worried."

"Come." Eldan holds the door open. "Let's go up to my rooms."

Devon eyes him, but does as he requests. He walks slowly as Eldan catches up after sealing the door. They walk up the stairs together.

"Is it like, super-private up here?"

"Mmm, sort of," Eldan says. "I like my solitude, sometimes."

Eldan reaches for his door. "Come on in."

Eldan uses the first room for spellwork, and so it has a large, battered wooden table in the center and shelves holding various ingredients and implements along one wall.

He heads to a door toward the back left of the room, which leads them into his living room. It's the same jumble of unmatched furniture as in Devon's apartment gathered around a fake fireplace that heats the room and flickers red light bulbs under a fake log. He'd found it charming and secured it for himself, and it almost looks like a real fireplace if one squints.

"Sit." Eldan takes a chair and smiles as Devon settles himself along the arm of the plush couch nearest to Eldan.

"So what's going on?" Devon asks. "Why am I up here?"

"I suppose I simply got lonely," Eldan says, shrugging. "I need to think, but my head has been rather uncooperative."

"I've been there," Devon says, raising his eyebrows and blinking. He sighs. "So. Your head won't work. What's next, then?"

"Ah, right to the point," Eldan says, cupping his own cheek and resting his elbow on the arm of the chair. "Well. That is where I am lost in conundrum."

"Well, how about you talk to me?" Devon asks. "I assume that's why I'm here?"

"Perhaps you could offer a fresh perspective?"

"Okay. Go for it."

"I shall," Eldan says, shifting a little to get comfortable. He draws his legs up under him and leans on the arm of the chair, closer to Devon. "Now. I have told you before that there are, *were* two havens in the Western Hemisphere?"

"Yours, and... what was her name?

"Imanja," Eldan says. "She was a goddess in her own right, an *orisha*. Very, very powerful. She preferred to stay on this plane, where she had believers, at least back when gods had credence and she could pose as one. Her haven was huge, but secret. Until now."

"They were killed?"

"Cristiano says some fanatic religious types followed one of them and managed to pierce the protection spells. We'll find out more from our friend when he arrives, I'm assuming. But everyone who was in the haven at the time was slaughtered, burned right inside their very own safety zone."

Devon's eyes go wide and he drops forward, elbows onto his knees, putting his face lower and looking up at Eldan. "That's horrifying."

"Yes, yes it is."

They sit in silence. It's not a comfortable silence, but for Eldan it is necessary to gather himself. What's happened is a tragedy: So many lives lost for nothing, over religious differences and prejudice against their kind. They deserve the respect of a few moments of silence, and Devon, all thanks be to him, understands that. He just nods quietly at the floor, and Eldan couldn't be more grateful.

"Now we need to figure out our next step," Eldan says, when his heart tells him enough time has passed. "And frankly, I have no idea what that should be. What step could possibly be taken after such a catastrophe?"

"You're already preparing for survivors," Devon says carefully. "Is there anything more to be done? I don't, there's no way to fight back from here—"

Eldan laughs, bitter and sudden. "Fight? You obviously don't know the Fae. We've been running away from a fight with the humans since they moved out of their caves and started settling. Ever since, they have conquered every piece of land they could get their hands on, and have had no regard for what might have already lived there. They simply took over, and we moved farther and farther inward, and look at us. Cramped into the tiniest of safe spaces, or spread out and solitary and struggling on the edges. That's those of us who *deign* to stay here, where we *have* to. The Queens are safe; what do the rabble matter?"

Devon gives him a sympathetic look. "I can't even think of what to say. What *can* we do?"

Eldan shrugs. "We can prepare for the worst. There's always a chance this will have further effects in the world. People might get suspicious. We could be discovered. And if that happens, the whole *world* will feel the blowback. I can't help but think that this should be brought to the Queens' attention."

"So why not do it?" Devon asks.

"Oh, several reasons," Eldan says. What to say about the Queens to someone who didn't grow up fearing and revering their absolute power? "First is that the Queens are entirely unpredictable. There's no telling what their response might be. And they might not take kindly to being bothered with something they could very well see as a trifle."

"A trifle?"

"Oh, yes. What do they care about a few hundred lives that aren't under their direct rule? Their subjects, yes, but only peasants, as it were. Only Imanja mattered, the only Lady, and she never lived as an obedient servant as she should have. She lived under her own authority, so what do the Queens care about her? What would they care about me? I'm hardly at Imanja's level when it comes to esteem and power, and I'm living outside of their influence. They may very well laugh me away, or worse."

"But this affects everybody," Devon insists. "All of them. What if the humans find out about Fae? That they're real. What if they get proof and go looking for the Queens?"

"Well, for the most part they have no magic, so they won't be able to cross over to get to them," Eldan says. "The worst case scenario will be an end to contact between Summerland and here. That means no help from the other side. No rule from the Lords. There are still Fae communities who live on this world and are under a Lord's care. They'd be abandoned, cut off from Summerland's magic and influence. They'd be no better than Céilí, havens that scrape the edges, and if the humans are looking for them, they'll find and destroy them."

"Okay, okay." Devon holds up his hands and shifts forward on his seat, leaning toward Eldan. "Look. That's the worst case scenario. How likely is it that that will happen?"

"It depends on how the Brazilian government handles the situation," Eldan says, grateful for a question he knows how to answer. "If they investigate, they will find inconsistencies. Some of the bodies might not be entirely human. They could be written off, ignored as freaks of nature. Or they could be looked into. There will also be magic left over, and who knows how that will appear now that it has no one controlling it. If the humans figure out a way to harness it, they could figure out how to use it."

"But humans can't use magic."

"Not necessarily true," Eldan says. "They just don't have it naturally. They can be sensitive to it, can harness and use it if they're sensitive enough. They can steal it, or it can be given to them. It's hard to do, but they can use magic."

"But the likelihood of that is hardly high," Devon says. "People will make an excuse for what they can't understand."

"Now?" Eldan says, shrugging. "Fifty years ago I'd agree and let it go. But humans are more and more open to the impossible. There's no telling what they'll do if they figure out that there are people living among them who are *different*. They don't have a good history in dealing well with outsiders."

"Okay. So then we have to prepare," Devon says. "What would be the worst case scenario in telling the Queens?"

Eldan considers. The Queens are most likely to maintain distance: What do they care if a few stragglers die off? But there's always a chance they will see it as a security breach. After all, if humans can harness power, they might be able to incorporate it into themselves well enough to use portals, and then Summerland would be in danger. It's all theoretical, but theories can be enough.

"Worst case, absolute worst case..." Eldan sighs. "The Queens send their Knights to eradicate us as a threat to the security of Summerland."

"Knights?"

Eldan blinks, and then remembers that Devon is still new to this. "Yes. Humans who work for the Queens. Liaisons to this world. They wield all the power of the Queens on Earth. They're the Queens' odd job men; they handle everything from soldiers' work to peace treaties. Word is they're rather influential among some of this world's governments, but we can only hope."

"Hope? That would be a good thing?"

"Well, if they're part of the Brazilian government, yes," Eldan says. "Then the investigation will already be taken care of."

"Maybe the Queens just need to hear about it to get that rolling. Eldan, it sounds like you might have to tell them. It sounds like you *should*. They're still the Queens, right? Like, they make the decisions."

"Yes and no," Eldan says, putting his feet back on the ground and shifting forward in his seat. He needs to be near Devon for this, for him to understand. "I'm out here on my own, remember?"

"Not on your own," Devon says, taking Eldan's hand. "You've got all of us."

Eldan's eyes prickle. Hell, he cannot cry just like this. He doesn't want to seem a fool in front of Devon. He sniffs and swallows. "Thank you."

Devon smiles and releases Eldan's hand, and Eldan wishes that he hadn't let go.

"Well, in any case," Eldan says, "I suppose I will have to contact the Queens. The question is when."

"When?"

"I can do it as soon as possible, or I can wait for more information."

"Your friend is coming, right?"

"Yes. Cristiano," Eldan says. "He'll be here in the next couple of days, if all goes well for him. Let's hope so."

"So, wait, or not? Couple of days isn't much."

"But they could mean something, if we're right about the Queens' fingers in the right pies."

"So?"

"So..."

So. Eldan will need all the power he can get his hands on. He'll need ingredients for the right spells and mana from Serena and help. He could ask for help, from someone whose magic is compatible with his own. Someone like Serena, or like Devon, perhaps?

Eldan grins. "So, would you like to help me do some rather impressive magic?"

HELPING ELDAN WORK THROUGH HIS issues felt good. Devon would never admit it, but he feels *special:* Eldan chose him to talk to. Not Kelsi. Not any of the others who have been here longer. *Him.*

He feels so special, so chosen. He might as well be a blushing teenager who got picked by the popular kid to be on the dodgeball team. And is it any wonder? He started as completely chosen: His parents chose him, chose to ask for him, chose to keep him. He knows that now, after an entire life wondering if his parents really wanted him. Devon was raised by music and TV and a long line of babysitters while his parents worked. Devon can't ache about that anymore, not after finding out that they chose him, they wanted him. Somewhere along the way, they put other priorities first. He believed that for his whole life he was on the edges, casually floating by, never making deep connections. And he doesn't feel up to connecting with his parents *now.*

Now he's making connections elsewhere. And Eldan is the deepest connection of all. It goes beyond their mentor-student relationship. They're friends. Devon has shared time with Eldan, just *being,* and that's not a luxury he's had before. He's incredibly attracted to Eldan, and there's no denying that. And Eldan returns it. Eldan, who no longer messes around after Devon disapproved. Is Eldan preparing for him, somehow? Making himself accessible, attractive to Devon?

A beautiful, funny, intelligent, fascinating man may very well *like* him. Blushing teenager, indeed.

And now Devon is going to see him do some magic and *help.* Real, flashy magic. Not invisible mind-games, not subtle flicks of a curtain. Real fucking *magic.* That is undeniably cool, and Devon is excited about it.

He mills around the bar while Eldan *prepares*. Devon's drinking some of his favorite cider, to build up his mana, as instructed. Everyone is doing something. Eldan watches them and sips away.

"Hey you," Kelsi says, retying her dreads into a high tail as she passes by. She's been busy with the people who camped out on stage, some ten or twelve people who stayed after the bad news. Devon wonders if this is the first pause in her day. "You and Eldan were up there a while."

"Talking," Devon says, perhaps a little too quickly. "He just wanted to talk."

Kelsi blinks and nods slowly. "Uh huh. Okay then."

"I'm serious. Just talking."

Kelsi nods again. "Okay." She eyes him. "Did you talk about mates like I said?"

Devon bites his lip. "Um. Not yet. Didn't seem like the right time."

She nods a third time. "Well. No rush. Not right now, not with, you know."

"Everything."

"Yeah," she laughs. "Everything."

Devon smiles, but awkwardness descends. He shuffles his feet.

"Are you waiting for him?" Kelsi asks.

"Yeah. I'm gonna help him with this thing."

Kelsi eyes him. "A thing."

"Yeah."

"His thing."

"Kelsi!"

"I'm just saying," she says, throwing her hands up. "It's something that's coming, you know? You and him."

Devon isn't sure how to react. His heart flutters fiercely, a feeling he's not sure he wants to dissect. "You sound so sure."

"I could be clairvoyant."

Oh. "Really? I didn't—" Kelsi is smiling a little too tightly, as if she's holding back laughter. "Oh. You're not, are you?"

"No. But I don't have to be. I know Eldan and I know how long he's been looking for a real connection. And I know the look you get on your face every time he talks. It'll happen."

"Devon?"

Devon turns, and Eldan, tall, beautiful Eldan, waits for him right there with a hopeful look on his face.

"Are you ready?" Eldan asks. "I'm rather brimming right now myself, so it's time."

"What are you two up to?" Kelsi asks.

"I'm making a call, my dear," Eldan says. "It's time we brought this to a higher authority. But keep everyone calm, please. I will handle this."

"I think I'll just keep it quiet, then, till it's over," Kelsi says. "Go, before more people figure it out or overhear."

"Devon? Shall we go?"

Eldan holds out his hand, and Devon lets him slide that hand around his back and gently usher him to the back room, through which a door leads to the private staircase to Eldan's rooms. They take it, and at the top Eldan pauses.

"Eldan?"

Eldan smiles wanly. "Yes. Simply preparing myself."

He draws himself up and strides ahead. He opens the door, and Devon follows.

Eldan has indeed been busy. While Devon was having his drink, Eldan set up the great table in his dining room with all kinds of *stuff*. Four bowls, one on each corner of the table, each filled with something different: one with dirt, one with water, one with sticks and one, to all appearances, empty. A circle is drawn around the table in chalk, and at the center is a round mirror about the size of a pizza pan.

Eldan steps up to the front of the table.

"This is where we'll do the spell," Eldan says. "I can open the channel easily enough, but I'd like you to assist in keeping it open. Stand behind me when I tell you to and put your hands on my shoulders. If we're compatible, I'll be able to take some of your energy to bolster mine, just enough to maintain a stronger connection than I would on my own, all right? You might get a little dizzy, but I promise you'll be okay."

"I'm not afraid, Eldan." Devon is excited to see this magic performed, to see the *Queens. What will they be like, these women that Eldan is wary to speak of?*

"No. You aren't, are you?" Eldan smiles. "Well. Best get on with it then. Stand nearby, please?"

Devon settles himself just behind Eldan, and Eldan nods. Then, he pulls a little vial from his pocket and shakes it.

"Here we go."

He uncorks the bottle, and Devon smells something almost metallic. Eldan walks to the first corner of the table, to the right, and pours a drop of whatever's inside the vial over the little pile of dirt.

"*Cré.*" His hand hovers over the bowl, and the dirt spreads and forms a flat plane under his palm. Eldan smiles and walks on.

He walks to the back right of the table and pours a drop into the empty bowl. "*Aer,*" he says and his hand hovers. The bowl trembles, and the dust motes in the air within it coalesce and spin. He walks on.

The third bowl holds sticks, and Eldan pours the liquid on them before hovering his hand, causing them to burst into flames. "*Tine.*" Devon can't help but push his breath out and shake his head. This is *cool*. All this magic, it's really *real*. He thought it was a story for children, but magic is *real*, and he's a part of it. He never thought much about fairytales but now he wishes he had, because it would make this moment *so much better*.

Finally, Eldan pours into the fourth bowl, filled with water, and his hand hovering creates little waves that splash on the sides of the bowl gently, as though upset. "*Uisce,*" he says and then he walks on.

He circles the table counter-clockwise three times and, when he reaches the head of the table once more, he nods to Devon. "Now."

Devon steps up as Eldan turns away and puts his hands on Eldan's slim, strong shoulders. Immediately, his palms tingle, as Eldan waves a hand. The mirror in the center of the table stands up, reflecting them. Eldan presses a palm to the center of it.

"*Oscailt agus a léiriú,*" Eldan says. Devon wishes he knew what the hell he was saying, but it's pretty, in any case. Celtic? Gaelic? Something. "*Na Ríona I Talún Samhraidh.*"

The mirror *clouds*, and Devon licks his lips and stands on his tiptoes to see over Eldan's shoulder. Nothing happens, though, for long moments, in which Eldan's breathing comes quick and loud. Devon squeezes his shoulders, and

Eldan whimpers faintly. But he slows down, and Devon keeps squeezing, staring at what he can see of Eldan's face, staring at the delicate line of his jaw, his high cheekbone, the flutter of an eyelash, the jut of his nose, which is freckled and fair.

But then the clouds part, and there they are.

Two women sit on thrones made of vines and flowers. On the left is a plump woman with skin so dark it's almost pitch black, with wild black hair clouding around her. She's robed in orange and smiles gently, like the Earth Mother made real. On the right sits a waif, platinum-haired and pale-eyed, with porcelain skin, clad in purple. She smiles even wider.

"Titania," Eldan says, nodding to the left. Then, to the right, "Mab. I greet you."

"You have been gone a long time," Titania says. Her voice is surprisingly sweet, but accented strangely. "You look well enough. So why do you call now?"

"Imanja is dead," Eldan says. "And all her haven, save one. Killed by humans."

"This is the risk she took," Mab says, her voice low and smooth.

"It's a risk for us all," Eldan counters softly.

"Even us? You are concerned for us?" Titania asks.

"And myself," Eldan says.

Titania smiles, revealing dimples. "You took your risks as well, my Lord."

Devon strains to listen. *Lord*? Eldan is a Lord?

"And they've paid off, so far," Eldan says. "I'd like that to continue."

"What do you want of us, Eldan?" Titania asks. "Protection, perhaps?"

"No," Eldan says. "I would never presume, my Queens. I ask guidance. I need to protect myself somehow. If I don't, and with the situation in Brazil, our nature might come to light. The humans might discover us."

"And? What do we care about the humans?" Mab says. She's like a corpse come to life, she's so cold and stiff and still. "What do we care for those who have shunned our light?"

"I do not shun you," Eldan protests. "I simply believe in something more from this world."

"We do not wish to argue," Titania says placidly. "Your beliefs are your own, and you are free to do as you wish with them. But why should we help you? The humans are not apt to believe in anything."

"You have connections to make sure they stay unbelieving," Eldan says. "You can make sure this stays an isolated incident."

"Control and power—there is none there," Mab says. "Chaos, like the darkness around stars."

"They won't stop with this world," Eldan warns. "It takes one to defect and reveal us. It takes one human to believe. It will end us."

"You threaten us," Mab spits.

"Do you?" Titania asks.

"Never," Eldan says. "I warn you. Our secrets cannot be kept. When your subjects fall, you lose your power, your control. And if the humans find a way to reach you where you are, if they learn from an errant Fae or a wizard or from Imanja's death, they will find you and they will destroy you. They will destroy us all; it is their most natural function."

Eldan pauses, and Devon can feel a sharp intake of breath.

"I see you having ideas," Titania says. She's unshakable. She remains good natured and calm. "Why must you keep yourself outside of my court? We would welcome you home. You could abandon your exile and return."

So it's true. Eldan's a Lord, from Summerland. He's not just a leader. He's something more.

"No," Eldan says. "My place is out here. Will you help me where I am?"

As Eldan asks, Devon's head lightens. He's woozy, uneasy. He gasps; nausea roils in his gut. He swallows it down and watches the Queens closely. *Don't lose it now.*

The Queens share a glance and then brush fingertips.

"We will consider it," Titania says. "Await our reply."

The mirror clouds again, and Eldan waves a hand. The mirror falls back to the table; in the bowls the elements fall inert. Devon steps back, releases Eldan's shoulders and promptly stumbles.

"Are you okay?" Eldan asks, suddenly there, grasping Devon's shoulders. "Devon?"

"'M okay," Devon says, very tired. "Just. Wow! That was—"

"I'm so sorry; you're drained," Eldan says, cupping his cheek. "Poor Devon. Let's get you down to your room."

Devon lets Eldan keep an arm around his shoulders. He's warm, and Devon is chilly and fatigued.

"So how did you like your first glimpse of our Queens?" Eldan asks, as they make their way slowly down the stairs.

"They're beautiful," Devon says. "Will they help us?"

Eldan shifts them through to the interior of Devon's apartment before he answers.

"I don't know, Devon, I truly don't," he says, leading Devon to his bedroom and depositing him on the bed. "Now. Sleep. I took too much from you, and you need to restore yourself. In the morning we'll have breakfast together, and we can talk more."

"No, wait," Devon says. "I have—"

He doesn't have questions, really. But he doesn't want Eldan to leave. Eldan sits on the edge of the bed and smiles down at him.

"What is it?" Eldan asks.

"You're a Lord," Devon says. "You never said."

Eldan grimaces. "It's not something that matters, Devon. My power is greater than that of an average Fae, yes. And I had holdings in Summerland. But I don't anymore. I left it all behind when I came here."

Devon nods. "Okay. I just, I guess it's impressive."

Eldan chuckles. "Well. Anything else?"

Devon rolls onto his back and grins. He can only think of one thing to say now. "That was really cool. That magic."

Eldan laughs. "Yeah. It was pretty cool."

"Stay," Devon says. "Tell me how you did it?"

"My arts are mysterious and arcane," Eldan says. "Though we *are* compatible. But it would involve magical theory, and I am just so *bored* by that."

"There's magical theory?" Devon asks, foregoing questions about their compatibility for now. "Like, are there books on it?"

Eldan laughs again. "Go to sleep. I'll tell you more in the morning."

"Promise?"

Eldan nods. "Promise."

But Devon doesn't want to be *alone*. He wants Eldan to stay. And he's too tired to examine why; he just likes Eldan's company, and it makes him feel better. "You should stay and talk instead."

Eldan sighs and then stretches out alongside Devon. "Fine. You want to know exactly how magic works?"

"A magic portal, anyway," Devon says. "Why did you have the elements?"

"All right," Eldan sighs. "First, you have to realize, magic isn't *easy*—"

7

DEVON WAKES WITH AN ARM over his stomach and a head on his shoulder. Upon further inspection, there is also a leg tangled around his ankle. His foot is asleep, and he has morning breath. Thank every heaven there might have been or that might still be, he doesn't have morning wood. Because when he sees black hair and long limbs, he wouldn't have been surprised if his sleeping body took things into its own hands.

He takes stock of his memories. He remembers lying down with Eldan and talking about magic for quite a while, but then things get sort of fuzzy. He must have fallen asleep, tired out from the spell. And Eldan must have dozed off with him, because here he is.

And wow, that's a lot of information. First, he saw something that should have been impossible, *would* have been impossible a couple of months ago. But he saw it with his own eyes, and while Devon's on medication, it's not for hallucinations, so he can trust what he experienced. Unless he went crazy a few months ago, in which case he needs a hospital, and quick. But this is all so *real*, and Devon's sure he didn't go crazy. He's not sure his own mind could have dreamed all this up.

God, he helped a faerie cast a magic spell. And he's a faerie too, right? Or a Fae, or is there a difference? He's never been clear on that. Can there be changelings of different kinds of faerie, or Fae? Like, could a pixie leave a baby in the world, or only a faerie? Does it make a difference?

There are still so many *questions*. If he dreamed this up, he'd have the answers, wouldn't he?

Eldan stirs, groaning faintly. "Devon?"

"Yeah."

Eldan tilts up, smiling but clearly still groggy. "What time is it?"

"I don't know; my cell's in my pocket," Devon says.

"Well, pull it out."

"You're lying on that side."

"Oh." Eldan yawns and then sits up, stretching his arms out to the sides as he goes. "Oof. This bed is narrower than I'm used to."

"Especially with two people in it?" Devon asks, digging in his pocket for his phone. He pulls it out. The battery is low; he'll have to go back to his place for the charger, and new clothes, for that matter. "It's just after eight."

"Well, breakfast should be ready," Eldan says. "Shall we?"

"Can I get myself together first?" Devon asks. "I don't wake up smelling like roses."

"Oh, fine," Eldan says. "I suppose I should wash up as well. Meet you downstairs?"

"Yeah."

Devon needs alone time, to wonder about how easily they spent the night together. And it was *nice*, too. He slept so well and he was so *warm*. He forgot what sleeping next to someone was like, how much he missed it. Even his morning shower couldn't warm him as Eldan had, with just the breath and the heat of his body. Nothing else, just being there.

The memory of that body is what Devon clings to as he brings himself off in that shower, as his hand holds the place for Eldan's, as he pants and leans against the shower wall because he can't hold himself up. To be held, to be trusted through sleep, these things arouse Devon more than anything, anything except the heaviness of Eldan's body pressed against him. He comes harder than he does when he uses fantasies of a faceless lover tenderly making love to him. Now that lover has a face.

His feelings for Eldan are beyond complicated. Devon can't deny that he *likes* Eldan. He's been a generous host, an attentive teacher, a warm friend, a mentor. He's not a feckless playboy as Devon first thought. He's searching, as Devon is. Kelsi told him to ask about *mates*; is Eldan is searching for his soulmate?

Could they—?

Half-formed, the question sits on the edge of Devon's mind as he goes to breakfast, where Eldan is waiting for him with two fruit bowls.

"Be healthy with me," he says in greeting, and Devon plops down beside him and partakes readily.

"So what are your plans for today?" Devon asks.

"I'm going to do some extra spellwork today," Eldan says. "Just some added protection to our existing glamours. It's mostly sitting around mumbling while Serena summons the mana and funnels it to me. I have to get things exactly right, so I stay in the basement and in the quiet. I won't be around much unless I'm taking a break."

"That sounds terrible," Devon says. "But necessary."

"Got it in one." Eldan takes a bite of pineapple, which he really enjoys, judging by the way he smiles and moans. "Okay. And what are you doing today, Devon? Do you have work?"

"Well, it's Sunday, so I have a shift at the supermarket, but I'm gonna call it off," Devon says. "I do need to go back to my apartment to change clothes. And I'll bring my work stuff. I'll just head to work from here tomorrow morning."

"Ah, good," Eldan says, grinning at him. "I'm glad you're staying."

"Yeah, I'm needed," Devon says, half-questioningly, and Eldan nods. So he nods back, and finishes his breakfast. "So. I'll go do that."

"Let me fund you a cab," Eldan says. "Get you there and back faster. You'll be taking the bus most days, won't you? Where is your job?"

"Not far from the stadium," Devon says. "So it's past where I live. It's like an hour bus ride from here."

Eldan clucks his tongue. "All the more reason to quit and come live with us."

Devon finds himself agreeing, but it doesn't feel right to just plop himself in. He's working up to it in his own time and he's not ready to leave everything behind. So he says, "Yeah. I'll get around to it eventually."

Eldan smiles. "Well. The day awaits you. If you don't mind helping out around here?"

"I'll see what I can do," Devon says. "How am I going to pay for that cab?"

"I will do it. Hush," Eldan says. "Here." He rounds the bar and kneels. A few seconds later he pops up with a fifty dollar bill in his hand, which he hands over to Devon. "There. Covered. I'll take it out of your wages."

"I get wages?" Devon asks.

"Of course," Eldan says. "You'll get your first paycheck when I get around to payroll. Now go so you can get back."

Devon smiles, and Eldan smiles back. They stand there, smiling, and Devon starts to feel awkward.

"Okay then," he says. "Bye."

DEVON KEEPS THE CAB WAITING while he runs into his apartment and packs a bag: five shirts, three sets of jeans, some socks and underwear, his phone charger, his medication. He makes sure his wallet is on him. He checks the fridge to make sure nothing has rotted, and then he runs back out and tells the cabbie to take him back. He gets an eye roll for it, but he doesn't much care.

When he gets back to Céilí, Eldan is out of sight, probably in the basement with Serena already. But he spots Kelsi sitting at one of the tables with some paperwork; a huge carafe of coffee and a mug sit in front of her.

"Mind if I join you?" he asks, putting his bag in a chair and dropping down next to her without waiting for her to reply. "God, can I get some of that coffee, too?"

"You just want everything," Kelsi jokes, but she nods at the bar. "Mugs're underneath."

Devon jumps up and grabs one, and then drops back to his seat and pours himself a mug of coffee. "So what are you up to?"

"Payroll," Kelsi says. "Eldan asked me to cover it."

"Do you guys write actual checks and everything?"

"No," Kelsi laughs. "We pay cash. But we keep a thorough record of everything and we do require you to log hours. Not strictly, but we pay a set fee per show, and then hourly wages for other work done around the place. And we keep track of work; sometimes the sprites try to get away with free wages but we usually catch them."

"Do I have to be careful of them? They haven't been friendly like the others."

"No," Kelsi says. "They're harmless. They like to keep to themselves, so just leave them be and they'll leave you be. They're here for their own reasons."

"Eldan?"

Kelsi raises an eyebrow. "Got some vested interest, newbie?"

Devon blushes. "No."

"Uh huh. Tell me another one."

"Look, I don't know what's going on with us," Devon admits. "I just like to be around him, okay?"

"No harm in that. But be careful, yeah? Don't play with him."

"Yeah."

They sip their coffee in peace while Kelsi does her bookwork. Devon is comfortable enough, even with people milling around, sitting at different tables. He watches them. These are patrons who felt the need to stay after the other night, people he's come to recognize casually. And there are still sleeping bags set up on the stage. Shouldn't they find somewhere better? Don't they need to keep the stage open?

"Hey, Kelsi."

"Yeah."

"Is Céilí open?"

"Technically no," Kelsi says. "I mean, everyone's welcome to come in, but we're not *running*. Not shows, anyway. Bar's still here; we'll still do business when Brandon is around to serve drinks. But until Eldan gets himself together, we've got no leadership, so we're just kind of floating around. And we have nowhere else to put the interlopers."

"Why not divide them up among our apartments? Those of us who have them. Or other rooms. There are more than three floors to this place, right?"

"They're not clean," Kelsi says. "And I wouldn't put these people in my apartment. Most of them make a living as petty criminals. I wouldn't trust most of them, because they don't trust most of us."

"But what about an empty room?" Devon asks. "Could I clean one out?"

"You can feel free to try," Kelsi says. "It's gross up on the fourth floor; it's all dusty and abandoned. But if you clear out one of those rooms, that'll help out."

"I'll do that. Where are cleaning supplies?"

"Somewhere in the kitchen. Sorry, I don't do the cleaning; that's the sprites and Brandon."

"I'll see if I can find Brandon," Devon says, standing. "Or I'll ask Ruad; he might know."

"Careful interrupting him during his lunch prep. He'll chop you up with the onions if you slow him down."

"I'm aware. But thanks for the tip. I'll just—"

He looks around as he heads for the kitchen. Brandon is nowhere to be seen. In fact, Devon hardly notices him around unless it's at night. Maybe he has a job in the city, like Maia? Like Devon himself?

However, he finds Ruad, not chopping onions but pounding thin steaks even thinner before tossing them into a heaping pile.

"What do you want?" Ruad asks.

Devon smiles nervously. "Cleaning supplies."

Ruad scoffs and shakes his head, but he points behind him with his meat hammer before returning to the pulverization of the latest cutlet. "Through the storeroom. In the back, there's a sink and a cabinet. Get in and get out; I'm busy."

"Be nice, Ruad."

Devon turns, and Eldan is standing there, sipping at a drink. His cheeks are flushed; he's pretty like that, like a doll. He smiles at Devon.

"Cleaning supplies?"

"I'm cleaning out one of the rooms on the fourth floor," Devon says. "For the people staying for the situation, y'know."

"Ah," Eldan says. "Well, that's rather helpful. But you won't clean out one of those on your own in one day. I'll send the sprites with you; they're not doing anything much. Most likely hanging backstage gossiping." He rolls his eyes exaggeratedly. "Theater people."

Devon never did theater in high school or college. But theater kids are tight, right?

Is *he* a theater kid now that he's a performer here? Or does he have to wait till he's on the rota?

"I have an idea." Eldan approaches and lowers his voice. "I want *you* to try to get into their heads. *Subtly.*"

"How? I've barely managed doing it like I'm stabbing someone."

"But you have managed it," Eldan says. "Now you simply take the same principle and scale it back. You said you used an icicle, right?"

"Yes."

"So make the icicle *really, really tiny*." He walks closer, right into Devon's space, and he gestures with his long fingers. "Almost too small to see. Just the tiniest sliver. And you slide that in and watch it melt into their brains."

Devon is nervous, and not just because Eldan is almost right against him. *Won't they feel it? What will they do if he fumbles it?* "Why? What?"

"Just try," Eldan says, putting his hand on Devon's shoulder. "The worst that can happen is that they notice and tell you to knock it off. But at best, you get to tell them whatever you want."

"Whatever I want?"

"Whatever you want," Eldan says, grinning. "Give them something to talk about, perhaps?" He glances over at Ruad. "I'll keep one or two behind for you, yes? So platter the food buffet-style, rather than plating individually."

"How many are there?" Devon asks, realizing he doesn't know.

"Six," Eldan says. "Two boys, two girls, and two, well, let's call them *otherwise*. They don't like to fall into a binary."

Devon bursts with the question, *has* to ask it, finds himself asking it before he can even stop himself. "And you've been with all of them?"

Eldan blinks and then nods to the side. "I have been with two. You interrupted me with two more, one of whom was rather hard to persuade, I might add. One has no interest in me whatsoever, and no interest in anyone, for that matter, as far as I understand, and the last one I've never had a chance with."

"Which two?"

Eldan eyes him. "Devon, I ache to ask, but what does it matter? I do not have any more to do with them outside of business. They are my friends and they have been here for me in my loneliest hours. Why make more of it?"

Devon swallows. "Sorry." He shouldn't have asked.

"I understand, I think," Eldan says, and one hand brushes against Devon's. "Feel free to talk to me, but, please understand in return. I've been looking a long time."

Devon's breathing is shallow. Eldan has been looking—for him, perhaps?

"We can talk later," Eldan whispers and then steps back. "I'll go let the sprites know. They will join you in the storeroom."

He turns, and then he's gone, leaving Devon standing, feeling somewhat winded. He turns to Ruad.

"Don't look at me," Ruad says. "I don't want to catch your lovesick."

"What—"

"Don't bother, boyo," Ruad says. "Just get your supplies and get out of my kitchen."

Devon throws out his hands, but doesn't fight it—the way Eldan left him feeling, the tingling in his arms and chest.

Let it be, for now. He and Eldan will talk later. For now, he has to get his supplies and get out, goddamnit.

The supply room is really a corner in the back of the storeroom. Past shelves of ingredients, fresh and canned and bottled, past boxes and bags, is a big metal sink and a janitorial mop bucket and mop, an industrial-sized broom and a metal cabinet full of cleaning supplies. He starts with the janitor's bucket. There's a hose attachment on the sink, so he positions it and turns on the hot water. Only then does he remember that he should put cleaning agent in the water. He pauses the flow, heads to the cabinet and searches until he grabs the right jug. With soap added, guesstimated, he turns the water back on.

The sprites walk in, four of them: two boys, a girl, and a fourth, genderless or genderful. Devon can't tell, and it's not his business. Zie has a long mane of hair in a mohawk that tilts over one side of zir head in a raven wave, and it compliments zir bone structure. The girl is a blonde, but fake, judging by her brown roots. The boys are brunettes, with identical faces and haircuts.

"Eldan said you need help," the girl says. Her voice is high and pretty. "We're cleaning?"

"Yeah," Devon says. "One of the rooms on the fourth floor."

The boys turn to each other and start whispering. Devon smiles.

"So," he says. "Just let me fill this up, and we can grab rags and the broom and go up?"

"Sure," the girl says, heading to the cabinet. She grabs a pile of rags and a bottle of window cleaner. The fourth sprite grabs more bottles of cleaning solutions and a couple of rolled up black trash bags, and then the boys grab the broom, which they thrust at Devon.

"We'll take the bucket," they say in unison, which is *creepy*, but kind of cool; are they twins? Or what, sextuplets? Six is sex, right?

"That looks full," the girl says, and she's right. Devon shuts off the water and then rolls the bucket toward the boys with the handle of the mop. They each take a handle and lift it easily.

"All right," Devon says. "Let's go."

THE FOURTH FLOOR IS *FILTHY*. In one of the large rooms, there are cobwebs, and dust lies thick on the floor. The windows are grimy, and bricks crumble from the walls and from the four pillars positioned around the room. It's a wreck, and it smells musty.

"Oh, shit," Devon says.

"The whole place started this gross," one of the boys says. "Eldan got it cleaned up."

"Were you with him then?"

"For the third floor," the other boy says. Then they set down the bucket and speak to one another quietly about getting another broom.

"Start with the cobwebs," the girl says. Devon *has* to learn these people's names. So he takes his broom, and then carefully imagines a very, very tiny icicle in his brain.

What's your name? he thinks, threading it into the vision of the icicle. *Tell me your name.*

Then he glances at the girl and sends the icicle at her, piercing her brain with it as gently as he can, just sliding it in between the lobes of her brain, as if it's insinuating itself inward.

She turns to him, and he smiles.

"I'm Kyla," she says, and Devon shivers. "The boys are Brendan and Brian, and then there's Niall."

"Devon," Devon replies, lifts the broom to catch the cobwebs and shakes them off onto the floor. "What are your other, um. The others' names?"

"We're family," Kyla says. "From the same tribe. My sister is Briana and my cousin's name is Shea."

"Well, nice to meet you," Devon says, with a question in his voice.

"You're Eldan's newest, aren't you?" Niall says, taking a rag from Kyla and scrubbing at the windows.

Devon forms another icicle, thinking *tell me about Eldan* and, as he slides it toward Kyla, he says, "Not exactly."

Kyla joins Niall at the windows. "Treat him right," she says. "Eldan is our patron. We owe him much."

"Yeah," Devon says. "I mean, I don't want to hurt him."

"Good."

She falls silent, and Devon won't push anymore, if this is all he's going to learn. Instead, he focuses on swiping away the cobwebs.

As he cleans, he starts to imagine that this is his life. This room, this empty room, left to gather dust, this is his life as it was, working two jobs, never getting his music out there, drifting like a mote in the midst of millions of others, just floating, hoping for some sunlight. But now he's got a chance to stir things up, to wipe away the dust and the grime and let that light in. It might be silly, but it warms him, that idea. He is fresher, more worthy of his own life, as though he's actually doing something with it. It's a good feeling.

So he cleans. He wipes away the cobwebs and dashes them to the floor. And then he pushes the broom against the dirt, gathering it into piles, which he can then sweep into a dustpan that Brian got when he saw Devon sweeping. And soon enough, the floor is bared: wood, plain and rough, but it's sturdy, it's something to work with. It can be washed, it can be made clean and whole again. It can be cleared of bricks and dirt and it can hold up a whole room. It's a good floor.

Devon's not thinking only of the floor. Not really.

By the time he finishes sweeping, the boys are mopping the other half of the room. Devon ties up his garbage bag and hauls it next to the second one, which is full of brick pieces and old, unusably dirty cleaning rags. The room is brighter, lighter already.

"I'll take these out," Devon says. "Is there a back door?"

"Go back to the supply corner; it's to the left," Niall says.

"Thanks."

He lifts the two bags, and they're not that heavy. One is full, the other about a third of the way, but there's nothing else to put in.

He gets downstairs, into the kitchen, and Ruad glares hard at him.

"Don't you get any dirt on my food," he says. "And bring up some lunch. I saved you some sandwiches." He shoves at him a plate with five sandwiches stacked on it.

"Thanks, Ruad," Devon says. "I'll get it after I toss these out."

Out back is a small enclosed area with one opening to the street off to the side. The gigantic bins are ready and waiting for garbage. Devon opens one and dumps the bags inside.

"You know, we have Ruad do a garbage run once a week so we don't have to pay municipal."

Devon jumps and turns. Eldan is standing at the back door, smiling in the afternoon sunlight.

"That so?" Devon says, wiping his brow.

"Oh yes," Eldan says. "Gets him out of that damn kitchen for a few hours every week. I'd say it's worth it. And he's the only one who can lift the bins."

"He's a big guy," Devon agrees. "How go the spells?"

"I'm taking a break," Eldan says. "Thought I'd come see the fourth floor, but I saw you heading out and I thought I'd ambush you."

"Success," Devon says. "You scared the hell out of me."

Eldan laughs and opens the back door. "Come on. Let's go see your work so you can clean up."

He wrinkles his nose, and Devon waves a dirty hand at Eldan's face. Eldan waves him away, faking a cough, and Devon laughs.

"Come on."

Ruad points at him as he passes by, and Devon nods and grabs the plate. "Thanks, Ruad!" And off they go.

Up the stairs, and Devon can't help but stare at Eldan's ass as he walks in front of him. It's a nice ass: perky, high and tight, just a bit round. He wears his jeans well, certainly. And by the way his hips sway, he knows Devon is looking: no way he usually walks that sensuously. How could he not notice this man?

At the top of the stairs, Eldan turns back and catches him staring.

"Hello," he says, wiggling his butt back and forth. "Can I help you?"

Devon blushes and buries his face in his free hand: a mistake, given the state of his hands. "Oh my god—"

"Ooh, don't ruin it for me," Eldan says. "Simply keep looking pretty. Come on, we're almost there, don't get *distracted* now."

He pulls open the door, and sunlight bursts through.

The room is *amazing*, compared to when they started. The floors are mopped, the windows are washed, the whole place is *clean*. It's not perfect, but it's suitable to live in, at least temporarily.

Eldan whistles. "Look at that. Couldn't have done it better myself."

"Except you already did," Devon counters. "You did this whole place by yourself."

"Well, not the third or fourth floors," Eldan says. "Anyway, yes, we can move up our temporary residents, I believe. And we'll have Brandon go out and get them a couple of space heaters. I don't think the vents reach this high."

The sprites nod, and Devon steps forward. "Food!"

They converge gratefully, reaching out and grabbing a steak sandwich each. They regroup by one of the pillars, leaning against it and conversing in low tones. Devon stands with Eldan; he shrugs, helpless.

"How did your experiment go?" Eldan asks quietly, as Devon picks up his sandwich and takes a bite.

He chews and swallows. "I got a few answers. Here and there."

"They're not very inclusive or forthcoming, I know," Eldan says. "But that's part of the fun. Getting them to come out of their shells."

"I only know a little bit," Devon says, trying not to imagine how Eldan knows so much. It makes him jealous, and he doesn't like that feeling. It's not a healthy feeling, not when he has no say in Eldan's life, past or present.

"Well, that's more than most," Eldan says. "You need a shower," he adds.

"Yes, I do," Devon says around a bite. He swallows again. "As soon as I'm done eating."

"And you'll have to change," Eldan says. "Laundry's in the basement. There's a schedule on the wall above the washing machine. Pencil yourself in where there's room."

Devon smiles. Warmth blooms in his chest and belly, as if he's swallowed something and it's spreading through him. Good whiskey, maybe. Speaking of which, do they even *have* whiskey? He'd like a glass sometime.

He decides to ask, sort of. He forms his icicle, *do you have whiskey?* and sends it to Eldan as quietly as he can.

Eldan raises an eyebrow. "That's you, isn't it?"

Devon smiles. "Maybe? How'd I do?"

"Pretty good," Eldan says. "Still could use a little more practice, but that was quite subtle. All of a sudden I started craving whiskey. I take it you want some?"

"I've got a hankering. Do you have it?"

"Not with mana in it," Eldan says. "Unfortunately that's not one of our infused drinks. But we do have some, I'm sure. But how are you going to *earn* it?"

Devon immediately suspects that Eldan is being suggestive. But Eldan simply smiles.

"Um. How?" Devon asks, finishing off his sandwich.

"Would you do me the honor of performing tonight?" Eldan says. "I'd like you to keep everyone calm. There's been some tension, today. A bit of contention between our residents and our guests, some rumors flying around, that sort of thing. You know how it goes when people are cramped together, yes?"

"I can imagine. Yeah, I'll perform a few songs if you want, try to tell them to be calm. How would I do that, though?"

Eldan considers him. "Why don't you tell me what you think you should do, theoretically? From what you know of magic and its workings?"

"Well. I know a lot of it is visualization. Mental power."

"Very good," Eldan says. "And so?"

"I need to visualize the mood in my music. In my words and my tone and my pitch."

"Okay. Tell me what you would visualize."

What would he visualize? Not an icicle. He has to do it to so many people at once, and he can't do it to each person individually; that would kill his focus. Just depend on what comes out of his mouth, so that whoever hears it gets the magic. So he has to work internally, really. Or, rather, internally to externally, that transition.

Maybe he can thread something into his words. Or coat them in something. Imagine them coming out like water, washing over the room he's in, and whatever dye he puts in it is the mood. To calm people? Maybe a cool blue, something soothing, like balm. Like ocean water.

"I'd imagine water," Devon says. "Like my words are like ocean water, and I'm washing it over everyone in the room."

Eldan nods thoughtfully. "That's a very interesting take."

"Are we done?" Kyla asks, wandering up. She stares intently at Devon.

Devon glances around and shrugs. "Uh. Yeah, I guess. Thanks for the help."

She nods at him, and then offers Eldan a wide, pretty smile, before turning back to her family. Together, they grab the supplies and head out of the room.

"Looks as if they've cleaned up," Eldan says, and it's true, they've left nothing behind for Devon.

"That was, wow!" Devon says. He raises his voice to the tail end of their group. "Thanks, guys!"

Eldan giggles and then smiles easily at Devon. "Time for a shower then?"

"Shower," Devon says. "Then I'll go see if Ruad needs help with dinner, and then performance?"

"We'll put you on first," Eldan says. "And tonight Kelsi and I will go over a new rota so you can be on a schedule. Part of the team, yes?"

"Thank you," Devon says. "Sincerely. Thank you."

"Of course," Eldan says. "You're one of us. We take care of our own." He turns and walks away, swaying his hips, and Devon will never live that down, will he? Still, it's nice to watch, and he might as well, if Eldan's got no problem with it. "Have a nice shower!" Eldan calls, and then he's gone.

A nice shower, indeed.

ONCE HE'S SHOWERED AND A little more *relaxed*, Devon heads down to the kitchen to help Ruad.

"What do you want?" Ruad asks genially, tossing a great deal of chopped up chicken in an oil and herb mixture with easy flicks of his thick wrists.

"Just seeing if you need help," Devon says.

"Could'a used you about twenty minutes ago," Ruad says. "When I was cutting up the chicken. Or forty minutes ago, when I was chopping the vegetables. Now? Not so much."

"So, what can I do?"

"Not my job to tell you. Find Eldan; I'm sure he's around somewhere."

Devon sighs and then nods. "Okay. Thanks anyway."

He heads out of the kitchen, and runs right into Brandon.

"Whoa!" Brandon says. "Easy there, buddy. Almost took me right out."

"Sorry. Just looking for Eldan."

Brandon smiles slowly. "Uh huh. What for?"

"I just need something to do," Devon says defensively. Why does everyone think— "He's the boss, right?"

"Yeah, but he's busy. Why don't you come help me? I've got to bottle some spirits for Serena while she's busy with her magic, and it'll go faster with two people."

That's as good a job as any. "Yeah. I'll help."

"Cool," Brandon says. "Just come with me."

He leads Devon through the kitchen and through a door to a stairway that leads into the basement. Devon whistles when he has a chance to look around.

"I know," Brandon says.

This is the distillery: big copper stills and pipes, barrels, at six stations down the line of the room, three on each side. Halfway down the room, in the middle of the concrete floor, a big slab is missing, revealing bare earth. In the middle of this sit Serena and Eldan, cross-legged, facing each other and holding hands. Eldan is murmuring lower than Devon can hear.

"Let's not disturb them," Brandon suggests, tugging on Devon's arm. "Let's go around and out."

He guides Devon around the wall, turning one corner. Halfway down, behind one of the big copper stills, is a door.

"Here we go," Brandon says. They enter a big room with huge shelves filled with wooden barrels on their sides. He heads to the farthest shelf. "Come help me with this. Damn heavy."

Devon helps him lift it down, and it is damn heavy. Together they lift it onto a big wooden table at the end of the room, next to which are two sets of shelves, one empty and one with the little wooden and glass spherical bottles in which Céilí keeps its home-brewed drinks.

"All right, let me just tap this," Brandon says, doing something complicated with a little spigot thing. "And here we go. Grab some glass, we're bottling bri today. Just fill 'em up and put 'em on the empty shelves to your right."

They gather some bottles, and then they get to work, taking turns to fill the bottles and then cork them from a little basket of corks. Soon enough, they have a rhythm going—Brandon fills, then stoppers while Devon fills, then Devon stoppers, and then Devon shelves both of their bottles while Brandon fills again. They work in silence for long minutes, fill cork pass shelve, fill cork pass shelve.

But then Brandon glances up and catches Devon's eye. "So. You and the boss."

"Nothing's happening," Devon says immediately.

"No, it's cool, man. Nothing happening yet, I get it. I don't partake of that sort of thing myself anyway, I get it. But you know. It's in the air."

"What is in the air?" Fill cork pass shelve. Fill cork pass shelve.

"Oh, you know," Brandon says. "Love. Sexual tension. Hormones. That sort of thing."

"Why is everyone so sure we're together?" Devon asks.

"Well, you guys did disappear together yesterday—"

"We talked! That's it!"

"Look, we're not used to Eldan disappearing with a pretty person to just *talk*, okay? This waiting-for-you thing he's doing is brand new. So we thought—he got you alone for the first time, right? And you guys have been all close with the training and stuff. And you look at each other like you want to eat each other's faces off when you're not staring at each other's asses. So, like, we thought you finally got it over with."

"No," Devon says. "We didn't."

"Well, you better be careful."

Devon raises an eyebrow. "I am?"

Brandon pauses and turns to face Devon. "Look, Eldan is important, okay? He's a Lord, he's our leader. Now, no offense, but we don't need some interloper coming along and breaking his heart, okay? I mean, you walk around here denying anything's happened like you're ashamed, and you want us to what, just trust you with him? You half-ass your way into joining us like we're the bad guys. You're never in a good mood. And yeah, you're talented and you've been helpful; you could really be one of us here. And Eldan is tripping over himself for you, and you treat it like it's offensive we'd think something was going on."

That makes Devon think. He doesn't find it *offensive*. He simply doesn't want people getting the wrong idea.

But then, why is it the wrong idea? Why does Devon feel uncomfortable when people assume they're together? It's not because he'd be *ashamed* to be with Eldan, no. Eldan is great...So why hasn't he made a move? And then, why hasn't Eldan? It's true, Devon rebuffed him once. He might be hesitant to make the first move, but Devon has shown himself receptive, hasn't he? He's moved here, he's helped out, he's been friendlier and he's opened up. Hasn't he? He's—he's quiet, but he hopes he's been demonstrative.

Maybe he doesn't want everyone thinking it's true before he's had the chance to experience it. It's as if they're getting joy out of it before he does, as if they're cheating him out of the pleasure.

"It's not like that," Devon says. "Look, I just, I want to be able to do this in my own time, okay? I don't want to jump into anything with things crazy like they are."

"Can I give you some advice?" Brandon asks. Devon nods. "It's never going to be a good time."

"Yeah. I guess."

But what does that mean? Never do it? Or do it now, because there's no time like the present?

"Look, we've got something done here," Brandon says. "Why don't you go catch some dinner while I finish up a few more bottles? You've got a performance tonight, I hear."

"Yeah, I do," Devon says, as nerves flutter in his stomach like moths. Butterflies are far too gentle to describe them, but moths bang into everything and, in Devon's opinion, that's a much more accurate description of stage nerves. And other nerves. He's got plenty to think about now. "I'll just—"

"Go, go."

ELDAN IS *TIRED*. WEARY, WEAK, bone-tired in a way he hasn't been in a long time. All that magic today, the wards and the glamours and the strength he poured into what was already up, it took a lot out of him. Gods, he is grateful for Ruad, who provides hearty meals, and for the sprites who serve him—Niall today, sweet thing, despite not wanting Eldan at all ever, brings him extra on his plate, and he starts scarfing down his chicken.

He's got a full mouth when Devon arrives, carrying his own plate.

"Mmmf," he says, as Devon approaches him. *So attractive; so eloquent.*

Devon laughs and takes his seat on the stool next to Eldan's chair. "That good, huh?"

Eldan swallows thickly. "I will have you know that I happen to be nourishing myself."

"Looks like," Devon says, with a little shit-eating grin, and Eldan cannot hate him, never. But then he takes his own bite and moans around it. "Mmm. That's—okay, I get it."

"Ruad knows his spices," Eldan says, taking another bite. "Mmm."

"What on Earth does he use?"

"He'll never tell you," Eldan says. "Don't ask him, either; he'll simply lie, and that would throw you off completely."

"Well, it's worth it, not knowing." Devon smiles. "How has your day been?"

Eldan warms because Devon is simply interested in his day. "Well, it was rather boring, actually. Lots of complicated spellwork. Weaving of energies, that sort of thing. I'm beat like a rather enthusiastically used drum, I'm afraid."

"I've known some drummers in my time," Devon says, nodding. "I can appreciate that."

"Hmm, well."

They eat in silence, and Eldan can sense tension coming from Devon. Eldan lets it go. If Devon has something he wants to talk about, he is perfectly free. Eldan will be here, available. And he won't push his own potential topics of conversation, their compatibility among them. It's a sign of something more, something deeper, Eldan is *sure* of it. But no, he won't push. Finally, Devon swallows a bite and sets his plate down and turns to Eldan.

"Eldan, can I ask you something? Um, unrelated to what we were talking about. It's kind of random, I just—"

"Yes, of course, Devon," Eldan interrupts, cutting off the babbling. "Whatever you'd like."

Devon fidgets. "I was talking to Kelsi a couple nights ago, and she said I should ask you about something."

Oh really? "Yes? What about?"

Devon bites his lip. "Um. Mates. She told me to ask you about mates."

Eldan's stomach does something rather unusual behind his sternum. If this is not a sign! "She *told* you to ask me? Why?"

The question clearly catches Devon off guard. He blinks, shakes his head, stares at the floor. "Just—um."

"I'm assuming you're reluctant to say because you were talking about me," Eldan guesses.

Devon winces. "Um. Yeah."

"Well, to avoid further awkwardness, I won't ask what you were saying," he offers, rather generously in his own opinion. "Was it at least good?"

"All good," Devon says; his relief is palpable. "So, what are mates? Like, soul mates?"

"Exactly so," Eldan says. "Though there's a little bit more to it. You see, some people are simply compatible, yes?"

"Yes."

"Well, that happens with magic as well," Eldan says. "Sometimes people simply match up. Their magic interacts well, their bodies, their *spirits*. And in our culture, we believe that that is more than compatibility. We believe that when someone matches us completely, magic and personality and all that, they are our mates. Meant to be ours. Like the Earth designed us for each other."

"I don't know if I believe all that," Devon says. "I mean, yeah, some people get along better than others. But to be designed that way?"

Eldan shrugs. "It's rare to find someone who matches you completely. Don't you think?"

"I don't know that it's possible at all."

"Ah, then we are at an impasse. Agree to disagree?"

"Why would Kelsi tell me to ask you that?" Devon says, and Eldan sighs. Damn Kelsi, sticking her nose in, but they *have* needed to talk about this.

"I don't know," Eldan decides to say. Less is better, when Eldan doesn't know a damn thing about how Devon feels or what he might be thinking. "Why don't you tell me, hm?"

"Uh, look, I just, I don't know," Devon stumbles. "Now probably isn't the best time for this conversation, is it—"

Eldan laughs. "And yet you picked it."

Devon runs a hand over his short hair. "I did, didn't I?" And then he laughs, light and silly, and Eldan's heart throbs in his chest. "When I helped you with your spell yesterday..."

Eldan can feel his heart in his chest. It's not any heavier, not any louder, but he's suddenly *aware* of it. It's there. It's beating.

"...were we compatible?"

Eldan nods. "Yes. We were. Or I would not have been able to draw from you and use it."

Devon nods. "I—"

"Hey, newbie. Get on stage."

Eldan shoots a glare, and it lands on Maia. She winces and gives him a questioning look, as though shocked and confused as to why Eldan would be looking at her like that. As if she didn't just interrupt—

"Yeah," Devon says, rising from his seat. "Yeah, I'm going."

He glances down at Eldan, wipes his palms on his pants and leaves, heading for the stage. As soon as he's gone, Eldan takes a piece of chicken from his plate and throws it at Maia.

"We were having a *moment*," Eldan hisses.

Maia shrugs and then kicks the chicken back at him before heading to the table at the front, leaving Eldan sitting alone. The room around him transitions into nighttime. The alcohol flows. Both Kelsi and Brandon are behind the bar. The place is almost full.

And Devon is on stage, sitting on his stool, holding a guitar. The lights look good on him. They warm him as they brighten him, and he belongs up here. He's assured as he's not off-stage, settled in his skin, as if the stage grounds him.

"Hi, everyone," Devon says into the mic. "I'm Devon."

He starts to pick out a slow, plaintive tune. And then he glances up at the crowd, and Eldan *feels* the music, as if he's put a cool washcloth over the back of his neck on a hot day. Eldan breathes, and Devon starts to sing.

> *I left my heart on the sidewalk*
> *Dropped the useless thing in the rain*
> *Got lost and wound up here with you*
> *Now I want it back again*

Devon shines when he sings. His low, easy voice melts over the crowd like bourbon over the ice of his magic. The ice soothes, the warmth relaxes, and Eldan can't help but laugh, because *his song is like Icy Hot.*

As he chuckles, Devon's eyes find his, and the humor falls away as their eyes lock. He's charmed and taken aback all at once by the intensity with which Devon sings to him, *just* to him.

> *So pick it up from the ground*
> *If you think it's worth the time*
> *I can't promise I can say much*
> *Without a tune or a rhyme*

And what can that mean? Has Eldan's waiting been rewarded? Their talk earlier, does it mean what he hopes? Devon's been less distant, yes, even *close*, but Eldan didn't think he was *ready* to move forward, if he were going to move forward at all. Or is he employing a performer's trick of picking one person in the audience to focus on? Is Eldan the easy choice, being in the back?

No. No, there's something here. There's heat in Devon's eyes as he sings. His lips curl around his words as if they're curling around smoke.

I'm not one for words
But if I could I'd say them to you
If I could write something down, or just come around
My thick tongue would speak true

And can the lyrics mean anything else? Why pick this song, with these words, with this meaning? Why sing it right to Eldan mere minutes after a conversation about mates? Why? This *means* something, and Eldan is through feeling like a fool over this man. He's finished with questioning; he can't anymore, he can't sit here uncertain.

This *is* about him. This *is* about *them*. And Eldan's going to do something about it.

The song ends, and Eldan is among the first to clap, but he's not alone. The whole place lights up with applause. So he stands, putting himself forward, and Devon looks right at him as he sets the guitar down and nods his head in acknowledgment of the applause. He doesn't look away.

Eldan waits as Devon hops off his stool, finally breaking eye contact to smile and converse with people up front who are vying for his attention. He stands, waiting, as the room returns to its normal chatter, until Devon finally makes his way through the crowd.

"Did you like it?" Devon asks, standing before Eldan with his hands over his pockets, rather than in them.

"You could've sung more than one song," Eldan says in reply. "One wasn't enough."

Devon licks his lips and then smiles softly. "There was only one song I wanted to sing."

Eldan steps forward, into Devon's space, and reaches for his hand.

"I liked it," Eldan says. "Very much. You are quite a performer."

Devon shrugs. "I just sang what I felt. I'm better at singing than I am at talking."

Eldan lifts their twined hands and kisses Devon's knuckles. "I have to say, I agree."

Devon laughs. "Okay, I deserved that." He steps closer to Eldan so their faces almost touch. "But I guess I'll have to do it anyway. We should talk about us sometime."

Eldan nods. "That would be good."

The tension rises as Eldan notices Devon's mouth, as their breath mingles. He can almost *feel* Devon breathing. But he has to go slowly. Eldan isn't sure what to trust; Devon could rebuff him again. And is this what he wants it to be? This is huge, and Eldan doesn't want to mess it up. So he drops Devon's hand and steps back.

"Um, Eldan?"

Eldan turns; Brandon waits for them to finish. "Yes, Brandon?" Devon sighs and runs a hand over his mouth, and Eldan's eyes are drawn to the movement.

"I'm sorry, man," Brandon says. "But there's a raven pecking its way around the kitchen. It got in when Ruad threw out the garbage from dinner, and it keeps cawing your name and sticking out its leg; it's super creepy—"

"A message," Eldan says. "From the Queens."

He glances at Devon, and shakes his head. *Later.*

"Show me."

THE MESSAGE SIMPLY READS *Now, as before*. Eldan doesn't have to be a genius to figure out that it means the same place as last time. He beckons to Devon, and up they go.

The mirror in the center of the table is already cloudy. He waves a hand, standing it on its end, and as soon as he does, the clouds clear, revealing the Queens in all their glory. His heart trembles; his fingertips quiver. His breath comes shorter; his chest aches. He can't stand the suspense.

But he can stand up to the Queens.

"We have come to a decision," Titania announces.

"Bear witness," Mab says.

Their hands are tangled between them; their eyes are both focused on Eldan, and Eldan can't help but feel the weight. These women are dangerous, far more dangerous than anything else he could face, and he exists on their whim alone. If they recall him, or if they have decided to destroy him using the Knights, there is nothing he can do against them. He can't defy them. And the possibility is now here, right in front of him. If Devon weren't at his back, he doesn't know if he could do it. He doesn't know if he could face the Queens.

"I bear witness," Eldan replies, keeping his back straight despite the urge to bow.

"We call no consequential action," Titania says. "You have chosen to live outside of our reach and therefore you shall be outside it. Our eyes remain but our hands withdraw. We are clean of this."

They fall silent, and Eldan's gut rings. Automatically, as though from a distance, he says, "Very well. Thank you." And that's it. The vision of the

Queens vanishes, and the mirror returns to its natural state. Eldan lowers it carefully.

This is the first time he's felt truly alone. He'd been separate from the Queens before, of course, but there has always been the possibility of the Court's support should things go awry. At the very least, a place to go afterward. But now he is *out of their reach* with only their eyes on him.

Eldan freezes. Isn't that curious? They said that their eyes were on him, didn't they?

"Eldan?"

Eldan turns, and Devon is still there. But this is important: They said their eyes *remain*—

"Eldan?"

Eldan shakes his head. "My apologies, Devon. That was rather a lot to process."

"Are you okay?" Devon asks, reaching a hand halfway out, as though unsure whether to offer it. Eldan takes it.

"I am pondering," Eldan says. "I admit I am disappointed that the Queens will not help in any way. But the thing is, the Queens *never* lie."

"Never?" Devon asks.

"Never," Eldan confirms. "They can't. It's not in their magic. They're the reasons for the human lore that says that the Fae cannot lie. Well, we can. It's uncommon in our culture, but we have the capacity. But not them. Do you see?"

"Not really," Devon says.

"They said their eyes would remain." Eldan takes Devon's other hand and holds Devon's gaze. "Devon. They have their eyes on us."

"Please explain to me what that means. I don't know what you're talking about."

"It means they've been watching us. They have an interest in us. It means, if I am not mistaken, that they have eyes *among* us. A spell would take too much to maintain. They have to have actual *eyes*."

"A spy?" Devon asks. "Is that—"

"It has to be," Eldan says. "And that means they have an interest, that means they aren't—"

And then it settles into his mind. The Queens have a spy watching him. It has to be someone he knows, someone he cares about. Someone has lied to him. And then Eldan's eyes flicker back to Devon. And who recently arrived, with no proof of his past, just settling in at the most *convenient* time?

"Devon," Eldan says. "Might I ask you to do something for me?"

"Sure," Devon says. "What do you need?"

Eldan squeezes his hands. "I need you to tell me again how you found Céilí."

Devon blinks. "I was wandering. And I kind of stumbled into it. Eldan? Eldan, do you—" He stops, gathering breath. "Eldan, you don't think *I'm*—"

"It would make the most sense, you must admit," Eldan says, drawing back his hands and staring Devon down. He has to face this, here and now.

His heart hurts in his chest. If it's true, he will have fallen for the cruelest subterfuge. He will have changed his heart for nothing, for a liar, a *spy*, for the *Queens*. And if he's working for the Queens, there's only one kind of person they send out on these missions. *The Knight*s. Eldan can't risk having the Knights around. Their work is dirty and they inevitably have blood on their hands; it's the nature of their work. The Queens send them out to do unspeakable things, and they simply cannot be trusted.

"Devon," Eldan says. "I'm afraid I must—"

"Let me prove it," Devon says, cutting him off. Eldan pauses. Devon's voice is desperate. How much does this mean to him? "Is there like, a spell? To tell if I'm lying?"

"No," Eldan says. And he has to wonder: *Is this man that good an actor? Can he be?* "No, there are no spells to detect lies. Only to confirm a truth."

"Okay. Then do it. I'll tell the truth, and you confirm it. I'm not the spy."

"Devon, it would take a very in-depth perusal of your mind. It's very difficult, and requires a lot of power. And I'd see everything in your head, every thought, every memory would be open for me to see. It can be painful and draining. Devon, are you sure you'd like to go through that?"

"You were going to ask me to leave, right?" Devon asks. Eldan won't lie, not now, considering everything. Even if it broke his heart, he would make Devon leave. He nods. "Okay. Then I want to do it."

"Devon—"

"You're all I have," Devon says, voice breaking. "Do it."

THEY SETTLE ON ELDAN'S COUCH, facing each other, each with one leg pulled up beneath them. Eldan holds out his hands, and Devon takes them readily.

"This may be uncomfortable," Eldan says. "It may even be frightening at times. You won't be in control of your own mind, your own memories. They'll come up without your bidding. But that's all that will happen. It'll be like a walk down memory lane. But it'll be me doing the walking."

Devon nods, but his eyes dart and his fingertips tremble. "Okay. I guess."

"Be sure about this, Devon," Eldan says. "I will see *everything*. Everything important, anyway. That means embarrassing moments, private moments. I'll see you with your boyfriends; I'll see you with your friends and family. I'll see all your lies, all your mistakes. I'll see *all* of it. Is that something you can take?"

Devon bites his lip and chews it, but then he nods, smiling faintly. "Yeah. Yeah, you can see it. I trust you."

The meaning of this does not escape Eldan. He senses that Devon doesn't trust like that easily, if ever.

"All right," Eldan says. "Come here."

He takes his hands from Devon's and places them on either side of Devon's head, with his palms cupping his cheeks and his fingertips in his hair, which is just long enough to start to curl prickly against Eldan's skin. His hands are buzzing already, as he rests his forehead against Devon's and closes his eyes.

Accessing Devon's mind is easy enough. On the outside, he doesn't give much away, but he's honest inside. He falls open like a sack of treasure dropped to the ground. Eldan imagines himself reaching into that treasure and sorting through it.

Memories are simple to pull up. People remember the important things easily, and he just has to coax Devon a little bit, remind him to remember. With a little magic between them, compatible as they are, Eldan sees as though they were his own memories: no explicit pictures, no sounds, just impressions of memories, like shapes in the darkness that is thought, but they're clear and bright, as though they really happened to him.

Images flash: sitting in a backyard, playing with a ball, grass around his small body, no one else in sight. A phone call, endless ringing on the other end. A hallway at a school, stark but filled with people. A meal around a table, the chatter indistinct and unimportant as Devon remains silent. A boy, handsome and achingly young, and the emotion felt in that moment as Devon formed his first crush. He feels the aching wish, for all of Devon's life, that someone would *see* him. That's all Devon wanted. For someone to *look*.

They go deeper. Eldan sees the crushes, the friendships half-formed and lost. He hears conversations never had with parents, things that Devon wanted to say and never did, and the things he wishes were said to him. He sees the first boyfriend, after college, the first time Devon held another man's hand in his own and knew it was right. He sees their first kiss and their first lovemaking, quick and sharp, as if the memories are important and cherished, kept in a protected part of the mind where they're fresh, like pictures kept in an album. Other memories float by, less well-preserved, as though left out of the album; the edges crumble, the colors blur and fade. But still, that *ache*, heavy and painful and draining.

And then Los Angeles. Mindless jobs, sprinkled with music on the edges. Songs partially written or fully realized, fingertips on guitar strings, calloused and familiar. Men, a few of them, each different, stark in their own ways. Devon doesn't take romance lightly, and no wonder. He has so little connection in his life. To open up enough to let someone in romantically is a special feat. But still, no one saw him.

Eldan understands that to him, connection *matters* because it's been so rare. Gods above and below, this man has lived most of his life lonely. And it's a loneliness Eldan recognizes in himself, come at from the other direction, perhaps, but the same in the end. Eldan has connected time and time again and made nothing solid. Devon has only connected a few times, but he's severed each one. They both end up the same, aching.

There is no deception here. He is who he says he is. Only recent memories remain.

What Eldan finds is himself. Céilí is warm around him, but he finds himself the focus of most of the memories. Perhaps it's because he's the one doing this, and Devon is aware of him. But no matter how deep he goes, he only finds himself. Yes, a connection has been made. It's not fully realized; it's being built piece by piece, but strength comes in careful formation. Devon is building something, not holding back. Eldan hadn't realized. He's been more receptive, that's true, but Eldan had no idea it went this deep in Devon's mind. He's shown Eldan rather than telling him, in some big ways. Moving here, helping, singing, letting himself be wooed in little ways. Devon is showing Eldan that he returns something of Eldan's feelings.

The only memories of the Queens are of the times he was with Eldan. And it doesn't matter how deep he goes, how much detail he pries from Devon's mind. Every last second he can recall, and nothing of being a spy.

Eldan eases himself away. He slows the memories bit by bit until Devon is in control, and then he pulls away completely. He blinks his eyes open, leans away, and gently removes his hands from Devon's head. He is sweating lightly, but Devon is trembling like a leaf.

"Oh no," Eldan says, immediately taking Devon's hands. "Did I hurt you?"

"I'm sorry," Devon says, voice breaking. "I'm sorry. That was really intense. So much I didn't even remember. And stuff, stuff I just hadn't thought about in a long time."

"I know that must have been intense. I'm so sorry to have to do that to you. But I know now, yes? I know who you are."

Devon's eyes spill over with tears. "I feel like an idiot."

"Never," Eldan says, reaching to wipe away the tears with the tenderest fingers he can manage. "Devon, you're more beautiful to me than you ever were. Don't apologize for feeling, please."

Devon laughs shakily. "I happen to know how red my eyes get, so don't start with me."

"No matter. Red is not unattractive."

Devon sighs and shakes his head, wiping his own eyes. "So. Now you know me."

"Now I know you," Eldan says, and the weight of it settles in his chest. He *knows* Devon now, probably better than anyone else. His knowledge of Devon is on par with Devon's own, and perhaps more accurate because he can see from a distance, unbiased.

That's a lie. He can't be unbiased. Eldan is in love with Devon, and that colors everything, especially his knowledge of their relationship. He's surer now that Devon is his mate. And with that, he has more strength than he ever had; he is more of himself. It's as if he's finally found a missing piece, a piece he could live without, certainly, but why would he? Why turn away from someone who is so well suited for him, destiny or no?

"Do you feel it too, Devon?" Eldan blurts. He can't not ask, not now. Not now that he's seen so far inside, seen that he's a part of Devon. He has to take this risk now, to settle his own heart. He *knows* Devon is as much a part of him as he is a part of Devon, and he wants to see their feelings through. The feelings ache in his stomach, in his heart. He can't *not* ask.

"Feel like you know me?" Devon asks.

Eldan takes his hands and squeezes them. "No. Not that I know you."

Devon meets his gaze, eyes only a little bit red, and they widen. "Oh."

"Mmm."

Devon blinks a few times, and then smiles shyly. "I think you know the answer to that."

Eldan bites his lip. He lifts his hand and cups Devon's cheek. He remembers the loneliness, the aching wish for someone to just *look*.

"I see you, Devon," he says gently. "I see you and I'm still here."

Devon's face is stunned, but then he crumples, and his breath catches in a sob. Eldan pulls him into his arms. He cries, and Eldan holds him, perfectly willing to weather this storm. Poor Devon. Eldan can only imagine what it must be like to have lived his life. But no more. Eldan will make sure of it.

Devon calms, and then sniffles as he pulls back. He shakes his head and wipes his eyes.

"Sorry."

"Never," Eldan says. "I am here. I said that."

"But you don't know the answer to who the spy is," Devon says. "We need to focus on that, remember?"

Ah, reason. "Yes, I suppose so. But are you okay?"

Devon nods. "With you, I am. So who do you think it might be?"

"I don't know," Eldan says. "After you, Brandon is the newest. So he's on the list. It could be, hell, it could be anyone, let's be honest. How much do you really know anyone? They're all capable."

"Even Kelsi?" Devon asks. "She's your best friend."

"She is. And my gut says no, it's not her. Nor Ruad; he's been in L.A. longer than I have, and has reason to be free of the Queens' influence."

"That narrows it down some," Devon says optimistically. "Can you do what you just did with me with everyone?"

"Ah," Eldan says. "Not really. It requires compatible magic. I'm not sure whom I'm compatible with. Serena at least, but it's, it's rather intrusive."

"But you didn't mind with me."

"I think we both know why, Devon. And you did consent."

"We know why I did that, too," Devon says. "Okay. So we don't know who it was. Can we watch closer now? Try to trick someone into revealing it?"

"We can," Eldan says. "I like the way you think. We need to do something big. And then we can see how people react. It's not *easy* to contact the Queens, even if the person doing it has a connection to them. They'd need spellwork, and only I have the necessary components to do that here at Céilí."

"Well, we'll have to keep an eye on people who live away from Céilí, then," Devon says. "What if they just go home and call up at the end of the night?"

"Ooh, no, I don't think so. They wouldn't be able to keep a close eye on me outside of Céilí. It's someone who lives here."

"Okay. So that narrows it down even more. Who's on the list?"

"The sprites," Eldan says. "Brandon. Serena. Maia. And, much as it pains me, Kelsi will have to be on the list. We can't discount her simply because I love her."

"I'm sorry," Devon says. Sweet, sweet boy. Eldan caresses the backs of Devon's knuckles with his thumbs.

"Don't be. That's a short list. We'll find whomever it is."

"So." Devon takes a breath. "What's your big move, then?"

Eldan slumps into the back of the couch. "I need to do something that would protect Céilí anyway. Something that would keep the humans out if they came calling."

"You've done all you can to keep them out. So. What if they do come in? What then?"

"We perish?" Eldan says. "I don't know. Clairvoyance isn't my strong suit."

"No, seriously," Devon says, hands taking Eldan's again, after they slipped away some time during the conversation. "Eldan, what if a human walked in right now. What would you do with him?"

Eldan almost scoffs; no human will just *walk* through his barriers. But Devon looks at him as if he understands something Eldan doesn't, so he frowns and considers.

"I would give him a drink, I guess," Eldan says. "Sit him down, and let him see the performance. I would act normally."

"Eldan, what if you did that anyway?"

Eldan's frown deepens. "You mean, what if—"

And then the vision blooms inside of him, and Eldan *gets it*.

"Are you saying," he says, hushed, "Devon, what if we opened up and *let* the world in?"

Devon nods frantically. "Yes. Eldan, yes."

"Hide in the open?" Eldan says. "Let them see us as harmless. Let them come to know us; let them *care* about us. What if we offer them what the rest of the world *can't*?"

"Don't tell them who we really are. Just give them a little taste of magic. Who could turn away from that?" Devon smiles. "I know I couldn't."

"Devon, you know that no Fae has ever tried anything like this, don't you? We stay hidden. We don't intermingle with humans."

"Except you *do*." Devon's eyes are bright and beautiful, looking into Eldan's own eyes. "*Changelings*. You put us into the human world to keep the bloodlines going. Why not make Céilí itself into a changeling?"

"Sneak it into human society." Eldan can't help it. He kisses Devon, just once, quick and firm. His lips are soft; his breath is sharply inhaled. It's *right*. But there are other matters at hand.

"Devon," he says, pulling back. "Devon, if this works, this could fix *everything*. This could keep us from *drowning*, this could make us a real, stable community. We wouldn't need to *hide* anymore. And it's, gods, it's a huge risk."

"But imagine pulling it off. Eldan, you could do it if anyone could."

"I have to take the risk," Eldan says, "but I need to think first. I need to think this through."

"Okay." Devon nods. "I don't have to be anywhere, if you'd like some company."

Eldan smiles. Beautiful, generous Devon. "Of course I'd love your company."

Devon stays still, and then grins at Eldan as he leans back against the arm of the couch and opens his arms. "Come rest with me. We both have a lot to think about."

Warmth blooms in Eldan's chest as he acquiesces. He lays himself down between Devon's legs, so that he's leaning back against Devon's chest. Devon's arms wrap themselves around Eldan, and Eldan's hands are splayed on the outsides of Devon's thighs. They settle, and Eldan closes his eyes.

Céilí as a changeling. It makes sense. Fae have been using changelings to keep magic alive in the human world for millennia. It's a natural part of their culture. Some mothers are willing to bear a child meant for the human world, and too-young or too-free mothers often choose to have their accidental children fostered by the humans. Changeling children may be given as gifts, or hidden away, or sometimes just left: the Fae's very own adoption system.

And what is Eldan himself but a lost child of the Fae hiding among humans? He left Summerland and his position at Court because he didn't agree with the Queens' politics. He alienated his fellow Lords and Ladies and eventually believed nothing was left to lose, but everything to gain. So he came to the human world and found his way to Los Angeles and made his own home.

What is he doing but keeping magic in the world? But he's hiding it instead of assimilating as a changeling does. He's keeping his magic locked away, just like Summerland. And he doesn't believe in Summerland anymore.

It's time to integrate himself into the culture in which he's chosen to live. It's time to open up and let the humans in, welcomed instead of barred, which will, he hopes, keep their suspicions at bay. And his people will still have a place. He will still serve mana infusions; he will still offer performances. He will still live up to the name of Céilí—a community celebration—except now his community will be wider. All of Los Angeles can come through his doors.

He's terribly excited. It's in a Fae's nature to love intrigue, to love stories, to love politics and challenges and the weaving of spells. Eldan will have to be the finest craftsman to mold Céilí into something appealing but commonplace enough to avoid close scrutiny, into something risky enough to attract humans, but safe for his people. He'll have to walk a tightrope. And Eldan *loves* heights.

He wants to start planning, and that means he needs the support of his people. It's time to let them know.

"Devon?" Eldan says, only just noticing that he himself is still smiling. He squeezes Devon's thighs. "Still with me?"

"Yeah." Devon's arms tighten around Eldan. "Just thinking."

"Me too," Eldan says. "I think I want to announce the opening of Céilí." Devon kisses his hair. "So do it."

Eldan springs up, then turns to offer Devon his hand.

"Come on. Finish your thinking downstairs. I'll announce it, and then we can finally bring this night to a close."

Eldan tugs Devon behind him to the door.

When they reach the bottom of the stairs, they hear loud chatter, louder than usual. Eldan opens the kitchen doors and sees a crowd of people near the front door.

"What's going on?" Devon asks. But Eldan can see a man: striking, dark, standing in the center of the crowd, smiling softly, a man he hasn't seen in perhaps ten years now, a man he's glad to see.

"It's Cristiano," Eldan says. "He's home."

9

CRISTIANO BEAMS AT ELDAN, AND Devon looks him over. He has dark skin and long, wavy hair. He's even shorter than Devon, wiry and thin. He's practically swallowed by the much taller Eldan when he throws himself into a hug.

"Eldan, it's been too long," Cristiano says, his voice accented. "Far too long."

"It's not my fault you were hiding in Brazil," Eldan says, holding the man back. "And never visited!"

"I was busy. So many foods to taste, so many men to kiss."

Eldan laughs. "I bet you excelled at both."

"Well, after the change, it got easier," Cristiano says, backing up and holding open his arms as though presenting himself. "How do I look?"

"Very nice," Eldan says, admiration clear in his voice. "Much different from when I last saw you. I assume you decided to complete your transition?"

"I've completed the spellwork. All done. I only take a potion now."

"Congratulations," Eldan says. "And are you still seducing poor forest folk into your embraces?"

"I haven't had to for at least a year. No point floating around like that if I can get what I want like this, hmm?"

Eldan finally remembers that Devon is there, apparently, because he suddenly turns his head. "Oh, Cristiano. Meet our newest member. This is Devon."

"Hi," Devon says.

"A changeling?" Cristiano asks. Devon nods, and Cristiano grins back at him. "I'm a *boto*. I turn into a dolphin."

"That's, that's cool," Devon says, not sure what else to say, but Cristiano just laughs and nods.

"Yeah, it is," he says. "So are you Eldan's new toy, or what?"

Devon's indignation rises. *Toy?*

"Ah, perhaps we should discuss this later," Eldan says. "Cristiano, be nice. It's not like that. But I have bigger news, and I have to announce it, so if you would be so kind as to drop it?"

"Sure thing," Cristiano says, hands up. "Sorry."

"I'll be back," Eldan says. He squeezes Devon's shoulder once. "Keep an eye on who reacts how, hmm?"

And then he slips away, leaving Cristiano and Devon standing awkwardly.

"Well," Cristiano says at length. "There go my chances of another shot with him. Congratulations."

Devon blinks and eyes this man. "Um. Thanks?"

Cristiano frowns. "Are you projecting?"

Devon freezes. What did Cristiano hear? Devon focuses on his shield, which has become almost second nature lately, and he does his best to reinforce it.

"I'm just getting a little bit," Cristiano says. "And you cut it off; you're good. But we're probably going to have to be careful around each other, eh?"

"Why?" Devon asks, wary.

"You push into other people's minds, yes?" Devon nods. Cristiano returns the gesture. "Well, I do the same thing. In another way than you do, though. You put yourself in. I take out. It's like I have better hearing than most. I can pick up what people think even behind their shields. What's muffled to others is not to me. Make sense? And your thoughts are louder than most people's. So it is double. Yeah?"

"I guess so," Devon worries because someone else might have access to his head. Eldan's already got to be careful to shield himself around Devon, because Eldan picks everything up anyway, and now someone else can do that to Devon?

"Well, we'd make a great team," Cristiano says, smirking. "You make a hole. I sneak in and grab. Yeah? Unless you and Eldan really are together."

Devon is trying to figuring out a response when a bit of feedback whines over the speakers. Eldan is on stage, tapping the mic.

"Hello," he says. "Everyone pay attention, please. I have an announcement to make."

He shakes out his hands gently at his sides, and Devon can see he's nervous. Without thinking, he reaches out, makes one of his icicles and threads it with all the encouragement he can muster. And he sees the moment Eldan feels it; he pauses, smiles and shakes his head, glancing up to find Devon's face. He straightens and then looks out at the crowd.

"We all know what happened in Brazil," he says. "The humans found where our people were hiding and they slaughtered us. And I refuse to let the same thing happen here. You all know we've been working on our protection, but I think it won't be enough."

A murmur susurrates, but Eldan isn't finished.

"We can't hide. We can't cower here under a shield that could fail at any moment. We need to stand up and face what's coming to us."

There's more outcry, but Eldan holds up his hands. "Hey! Listen! We're not going to fight!" The crowd settles, and Eldan smirks, drawing them all in. "We're not going to fight at all. No. We are Fae. We are going to *entertain*."

And Devon knows, now, the Fae code of hospitality. The legends and the myths of Fae trapping humans and playing tricks on them are all stories of Faerie power.

"We're going to open Céilí to the humans," Eldan says. "We're going to let them in. And we won't tell them anything more than necessary. No need. But if they know us, if we provide them with something they can't get anywhere else, they will *need* us. They will *trust* us. And when the time comes that our world can no longer be kept secret, they will remember all that Céilí has done for them and all the power we have, and they will welcome us.

"This is risky," he continues. "You know that. We'll be playing a dangerous game. But I believe that we can win that game. I believe we can pull off a stunt that even Mab and Titania have been afraid to try. We can let the human world in and we can adapt to their world, the world that has been pressing at us for *centuries*. And once we do that, we will rise again. Glory is not just in our past; it's ours for the taking once more. And I plan to take it right from the offered hands of the humans. If you aren't ready, you're welcome to leave, and I'll send you with my blessing for luck in finding a new safe haven. But I need as many of you as possible to pull this off."

He looks around at everyone in the room, taking his time, letting them murmur, before he says, "What do you say?"

Two people head for the door, and Eldan simply nods, as though he expected as much. But the rest of the room remains.

"You're with me?" Eldan asks, and someone starts to clap. It's taken up, and Eldan stands there under the applause.

"Your loyalty is appreciated, even if I know most of you are simply excited by the politics," he says, and the room laughs. "Free drinks, come on! We've got work coming our way; let's have a celebration!"

Devon, grinning in spite of himself, claps with the rest of the room, and by his side Cristiano whistles. Eldan waves to acknowledge them, but he's swallowed up by the crowd as soon as he's off stage.

"So, no kidding, huh?" Cristiano says. "You two. You had a moment."

Devon blushes. "Look—"

"Just saying, just saying," Cristiano says. "I'm not going to step in the way, promise. I'll find someone else for Beltane."

Devon frowns. *Beltane? What on earth is that?*

"I'm gonna get something to eat," Devon says. It's been a long, long night after all. He ate before his song on stage, but then there was the Queens' message, and then Eldan and the mental link. God, it's been a long, long night, and Devon doesn't even know what time it is. He's starving and he needs a drink and to sit the fuck down.

"I'll come with," Cristiano says. "I could use something."

Devon nods toward the kitchen. He's awkward with Cristiano there; he's obviously a previous lover of Eldan's, who hoped for more this time around. Only Devon's presence is stopping him. Cristiano is gorgeous and so far quite charming. Devon knows he's lacking in the easy magnetism that Cristiano clearly has in spades. It makes him a bit insecure, a bit uncertain, and he was feeling that way anyway, especially after Eldan kissed him and then lay in his arms.

And that kiss. Devon felt it in his *toes*. But it had been over so quickly, when all Devon wanted to do was continue. And now he's in limbo. He wants more, but he isn't able to get more. Devon knows logically that Cristiano won't usurp Eldan's affections, not after everything they've been through. And then there's the whole mates thing, which is still confusing and hard to believe.

But man, if they can kiss like that, if they can be in each other's arms, Devon will use any term Eldan wants.

For now, though, he finds Ruad wiping his knives in the kitchen.

"Dinner done?" Devon asks.

"Yes," Ruad says. "Stew's on, though. Bowls are on the shelf; ladle's on the side."

"Thanks, Ruad." Devon grabs the bowls and spoons and holds one set out for Cristiano.

"Get him out of my kitchen, though," Ruad says. "Soon as that bowl is filled, I want him out."

"Ruad," Cristiano says genially. "I promise not to knock anything over this time."

"You'll not do a damn thing," Ruad says, "because I'm not giving you the chance. Get your food and *out*."

Devon ladles himself some stew. It smells wonderful.

"Is the stew always on?" Devon asks.

Cristiano laughs behind him. Ruad just shrugs.

"It never ends," he says with a little smirk. Devon shakes his head. The mystery of the stew remains. He ladles some for Cristiano, too, and then hangs the ladle.

"Thanks, man," he says, heading out of the kitchen with Cristiano in tow.

At the bar, Brandon automatically pours him a glass of cider, along with one for Cristiano. Devon takes his with a grin and a little salute of the glass, then goes to the table where the Céilí crew sits.

Kelsi and Maia are conversing intently. He sits anyway, and smiles as Cristiano sits next to him. He's obviously attached to Devon for the night; he hasn't moved away from him since they were introduced.

"Look what we have here," Cristiano says. "Sister! I missed you!"

"Go fuck yourself, Cris," Maia says. "I was in the middle of a conversation."

"But I am here," Cristiano says. "Greet me. You did not greet me before."

"Hello, Cristiano," she says. "Now shut up and eat your food."

Cristiano chuckles, turning to Devon. "I enjoy teasing her. She is easy to rile up."

"I noticed," Devon says. "She's your sister?"

"Not by blood," Cristiano says. "But we are the same, she and I. We both take mana from others. Leeches, the both of us."

"I can hear you," Maia says. "Did you really just call me a leech?"

"The truth is the truth," Cristiano says. "We suck the life from our victims."

"We suck *mana* from our victims," Maia sneers. Devon, finding this distasteful, must be making a face, because Maia glances at him and then rolls her eyes. "It's like milking a cow. You make more and it won't kill you."

"Moo," Cristiano says in Devon's ear. Startled, Devon laughs once.

"Ignore him," Maia says, turning back to Kelsi.

Devon eats in peace until the lights go down. In skimpy outfits, three of the sprites, whose names he can't remember aside from Kyla, assemble onstage. One is Kyla's sister—Briana?—but the third is the cousin, what is zir name?

The dancing is classic burlesque: lots of wiggling and snapping and twisting and chairs. Except that it's obviously pretty, Devon can't tell a damn thing about it. It is probably good. It's certainly very sinuous.

By the end of the set, he's finished his meal and his drink, and so has Cristiano.

"They are good," Cristiano says, nodding as the dancers file off stage to smatterings of applause. "I missed seeing them."

"How long have you been gone?" Devon asks.

"Oh, eight years? Seven? Not too long ago."

Eight years ago was still high school to Devon. It hits him how young he really is among these people, practically a child.

He's at a loss for a real response.

But before any response need be made, Eldan makes his way through the crowd and claps a hand on each of their shoulders.

"You two," he says. "I need a word."

ELDAN SHUTS THE CURTAIN BEHIND them and waves his hand, so Devon assumes the curtain is now rigidly solid. Then, Eldan sits on his throne and beckons to them.

"I have need of you. Cristiano, this will fill you in; Devon, you already know. Someone among us is spying for the Queens. I intend to find out who it is."

"How do we know it's not him?" Devon asks, nodding over at Cristiano. He figures if he's going to have to trust this guy, he has a right to know.

"Because what spy would be missing for eight years?" Cristiano points out.

"Could've been spying on—on Imanja," Devon says, stumbling over the name. "And now Eldan is interesting again."

"Fair point," Eldan says. "But we're working on the assumption that the spy is already amongst us. Cristiano only just arrived. And, if we don't find the spy elsewhere, we'll know anyway, yes? So, Cristiano, better find that spy with us, yes?"

"I will do my best," Cristiano says, smirking.

He's getting on Devon's nerves, but Devon realizes that it's probably due to jealousy. He is *just* getting used to the idea that he and Eldan might be together, and he's waiting for this crisis to pass. This limbo isn't a comfortable place, and Cristiano, with his charisma and his good looks and his previous relationship with Eldan is not helping at all.

"And you?" Eldan is asking, as Devon reaches his internal conclusion.

"I'm in," he says. "Just tell me what you need me to do."

"We're going to stage this as a series of interviews," Eldan says. "We'll need new acts, new drinks, new menu, new everything. So we'll bring in our regular crew one by one to get their ideas. Devon, you will be suggesting that each of them lower their shields. Just a touch, get them to relax. Then, Cristiano will try to nab information on any spying."

"Isn't that too invasive?" Devon asks.

Eldan sighs. "I don't like it any more than you do, but we need to have an advantage. I want information before I act, and if we ask outright, we'll simply send the spy into further hiding. We want whomever it is relaxed and ready to give up information."

"That we're going to steal from them," Devon says. But he holds up a hand and sighs himself. "No, I get it. Morals aside, I'll trust this is the best option. I don't understand your politics; I'm just a soldier here, right?"

Eldan grimaces. "I like it even less than before when you put it that way."

"Look, I won't go deep," Cristiano says. "If it's the spy, chances are the shield will be phenomenal. I'll know it's suspicious if I can't get in at all, okay? So I won't probe hard. Just hard enough to see if they're hiding something."

"We can try it that way," Eldan says. "Devon, does that ease your mind at all?"

Devon nods. "Yeah. That feels less—you know."

"I think I understand, yes," Eldan says. "Well. Shall we start tomorrow morning? It's rather late to do it tonight, and I have been remiss in planning for Beltane, so I have that to look forward to for the next several hours."

Cristiano whistles. "It's this weekend, Eldan."

"And today is Tuesday, yes, I know," Eldan says. "Like I said, remiss. But everything will be taken care of, and we'll have a grand celebration just like we always do."

"I look forward to it," Cristiano says. "Now. Let me find a bed for the night."

He winks, and Eldan laughs, waving a hand at the curtain. It falls soft, and Cristiano slips from the room without another word.

Devon turns back to Eldan. "Beltane?"

"Our spring festival," Eldan says. "A fertility rite, welcoming the new life, that sort of thing. Classically, we light two huge bonfires, and anyone who wants to be renewed walks between the bonfires to be blessed by their sacred light. And the old year falls away, and we're left with new selves."

To Devon, who has done much changing in the past couple of months, this is an appealing idea. "A fresh start?"

"That's right." Eldan stands and approaches Devon. "I was hoping you might attend with me. The activities can get rather boisterous, rather *raunchy* as well, and I'd like you to be by my side."

Eldan wants to be near him for the raunchy stuff, huh? Devon's gut warms pleasantly. "I think that can be arranged," he says. And because he cannot help his jealousy, "Unless Cristiano will be there."

Eldan raises an eyebrow. "Why, were you interested in him?"

"No," Devon says. "I just know that he hoped to know you better again."

Eldan takes Devon's hand in both of his own and brings it up for a light kiss. "Cristiano was a simple dalliance many, many years ago. And he'll remain just that. I have a mate, now, you see."

"I still don't quite know what that means."

"It means whatever we want it to mean. It means that our souls, our spirits, our mana, our very selves are suited to each other. We complement each other in a way that others can't, and it's very likely that we've met in other lives, and we'll continue to meet after this one. But that's simply how we're made. We can choose another path, separate paths. We always have a choice. But I choose you, Devon. May I ask if you say the same?"

It's a bold question, and Devon respects the hell out of Eldan. But his heart races faster than his mind, and he finds a lot more than respect. "I would like to."

"Then you can," Eldan says, stepping closer. Closer. *Closer*.

"Okay. I will."

He brings their mouths together. It's a stretch since Eldan is tall, but then Eldan's arm winds around Devon's lower back and supports him, and it's that much easier to just *lean* in, fall into Eldan's arms and let himself be kissed. Eldan kisses well: firm lips, soft tongue, moving like water in ebbs and flows. This is the kiss Devon wanted earlier; this is the kiss he needs now.

"Your room?" Devon asks breathlessly, as Eldan kisses along his jaw.

But Eldan stops.

"Perhaps—perhaps we should leave it here for tonight. I have this notion that we should wait to go further until after Beltane. Call me silly, but I'd like to feel purified before I claim you as mine. And I'd like to show you that this is not all I want you for."

Devon, who understands romance, finds this thrilling. Oh, he can wait— it'll be torture, but for a man like Eldan, he can wait less than one week.

"Okay," Devon says. "Till after Beltane, then."

10

THE WEEK PASSES EVEN MORE quickly than Devon hoped.

Devon quits his job at the supermarket. He doesn't give two weeks' notice. He just quits, and the management apparently has no hard feelings, because they offer to mail his final check. It's not a hard parting, and Devon wonders why he held on for so long.

The same cannot be said about his apartment, though. He's lived there since he moved to L.A., and it's his home. But he packs it up all the same. He only has the rest of this month and one more left on his lease, so he'll pay and be gone. He'll have the cash after his next paycheck, and it'll give him time to find a place for his furniture, either selling it or finding a place for it at Céilí.

Finally, he fills his prescription and calls his doctor to make sure he's scheduled for more, and then he gathers up his things and goes back to his new home.

ELDAN IS FINISHING A CUP of coffee when Devon comes in late that morning with three boxes and two duffle bags juggled in his arms.

"What is this?" Eldan asks.

"My shit," Devon says. "Anyone give me a hand?"

Eldan himself gives him that hand. He takes the three boxes and leaves Devon with the duffle bags, and then leads the way to Devon's apartment. Once they're inside, Eldan drops the boxes, pulls the duffle bags from Devon's arms, and pulls him in.

"You're here?" he asks between kisses, muffled by Devon's lips.

"I'm here," Devon gasps, and Eldan's hands on him are possessive and sure. Devon's body is tight underneath them, and warm and *real*. Eldan, now that he's convinced of their status as mates, can't quite believe it's real. He's been waiting hundreds of years, and it's finally here, what he's always wanted: the companionship, the *friendship*, the romance, the understanding and the closeness and the absolute connection. He felt it, surely, when they called the Queens the first time. Their magic acted as one so easily, as if they were made to mingle that way. Eldan *felt* it and he still feels it. It's overwhelming, especially as he's holding Devon against him, kissing him, feeling the softness of his lips and tongue and the hardness of his body.

But they're waiting. And when Eldan pulls back, it's not without frustration.

It's not the only thing frustrating Eldan, either. The interview process lasts almost the entire week, and with little result. Only two people stand out: Brandon, because his mind is almost blank when Cristiano probes at it, and Maia, because she catches them probing and throws a private but vicious fit.

"I'm saying it's her," Cristiano says. "Brandon's a simpleton, nothing more. But she's far too protective of her mind."

Eldan knows Maia, or he thinks he does. She is protective of herself. She has her reasons, but are they just excuses, really? Is it all part of a cover?

"Well, let's keep a closer eye on her, then," he says. "Now, about her performance slot—"

And it continues, amidst all the business of the place. They manage to do a lot toward opening Céilí. There's a whole new performance rota, and Eldan makes sure Devon has two nights to woo the crowds.

"You'll get more once you prove a hit," Eldan says, with no doubt that he will. "That's why we have that revolving spot on Fridays and the open slot on Sundays. We'll put Maia in there for now, keep her happy, but that gives her four performances. We'll let you have more when you're a little less green, yes?"

Devon's happy with that and with being the floater. He helps out bottling liquor, mostly with Brandon and occasionally with Serena, and taking inventory of their stores with Eldan himself. Some nights, he shadows Ruad as well, cleaning up after him when the meal is more complicated. Eldan keeps an eye on him and is proud of his resourcefulness and resilience. He's been through a lot and he's fitting in so beautifully. He belongs here, and Eldan's known from day one. Now that he's here for good, and his ties to the human world are fewer and weaker, Eldan can't help but feel happy.

And it all comes together on Saturday evening.

"That's it," Eldan says, checking off the last item on his to-do list. "We've got everything prepared for tonight, and planning for our opening is done. Now all that's left is to light the fires and have a party!"

"And wait for Ruad to finish the food," Devon reminds him. "He's not done yet."

"Well," Eldan says, sitting down on his throne. "Then let's relax. We can take a few minutes while Ruad finishes before we go up to the roof."

"What kind of glamour do you need to hide a huge bonfire?" Devon asks.

"A big one," Eldan says, smiling. "That's where I was all morning, extending the glamour into the sky. It'll cover the plume's location, and the smoke should look like a low, dark cloud when anybody sees it. Probably no one will notice. No one has, not in all my years here."

"And then we'll start changing the glamours," Devon says.

Eldan nods. "The construction site will start to look like there's progress. And then, eventually, we'll simply—poof, be done."

"How long?"

"Three months. So we can perfect our routines and get the fourth floor going for, you know, business meetings, that sort of thing."

"Private rooms," Devon corroborates. "I'll be helping out there a lot, I assume."

"You, the sprites and several of our regular customers have volunteered to help," Eldan says, nodding. "Kelsi will help too, when she has time, as will the rest of us."

"You should conserve your strength for the harder stuff. You're going to be doing so much with the glamours and the spellwork."

"The menial labor will be a nice break, trust me," Eldan says. "It'll be nice to move my body after being cramped up in that basement with Serena."

"Eldan." It's Cristiano, coming back from the kitchen. "Ruad says to get started. The sprites are going to be setting up any minute."

"Oh, good," Eldan says, hopping up from his chair. "Cristiano, if you would spread the word that we'll be up and ready in half an hour's time?" With that, he takes Devon's hand in his and tugs him to the stairs at a run.

Tonight is their night.

THE ROOF, ABOVE THE FOURTH floor, is huge and flat, with vents and such across it, but there's room for the two piles of wood. Devon eyes them.

"Ready to see something cool?" Eldan asks, rubbing his hands together.

"Always," Devon says, stepping back.

Eldan grins, wolfish and happy, and parts his hands. Between them, a little flame erupts, and before it can go out he tosses it at one of the piles of wood. It hits the kindling underneath and starts to crackle, catching the wood slowly.

"Okay, not as dramatic as I'd like," Eldan says. Devon holds back his laughter, though poorly, if Eldan's half-annoyed look is anything to go by. "Yeah, yeah. Just let me light the damn fires."

Devon laughs outright and grabs Eldan's shoulder with one hand. Eldan smiles down at him and kisses him before lighting the second fire. Within a few minutes, the fires have caught the bigger logs and burn brighter.

"And no one can see us up here," Devon says thoughtfully, looking out over the street. Cars go by, but it's not one of L.A.'s busiest streets.

Eldan circles Devon's shoulders with both arms and leans to rest his head against Devon's temple. "No. We're invisible."

"Good," Devon says, turning. "Then I can do this."

He catches Eldan's mouth against his own, and it's so good. Lips and tongue, increasingly passionate as they turn to face one another wholly, hands on each other, torsos rocking together and apart in the motion of it, until—

"Hey!" someone shouts. "The party hasn't started yet!"

Devon sighs, pulling back. It's Maia, holding up a beer bottle, which she then takes a swig from. Eldan laughs.

"We can slip away later," he whispers quickly. "After the ceremony. But do me a favor in the meantime?"

"What's that?"

"See if you can keep your mind on who's here and who's not? Let me know if anyone goes missing."

"I can try," Devon says, aware of the limitations of his powers. Sensing others isn't something he's very good at.

"I'll have Cristiano help you. Just get a feel for everyone as best you can."

Then, with a squeeze of hands, Eldan slips away, toward the two long tables set up with drinks and food.

Devon ambles over at his own pace and picks up a bottle of cider, one of the wooden orbs peculiar to Céilí. They're serving alcohol by the bottle tonight, and Devon's happy enough to swig directly from the source. He holds onto the bottle and hangs back, watching as everyone gathers into little groups.

Everyone's there, even people Devon hasn't seen before who apparently only come out for Beltane. Great. His job is that much harder.

"Don't worry about it," Cristiano says, appearing at his elbow. "We only need to keep an eye on the regular crew."

"How did you know I was worrying?" Devon asks.

"Your face, it did a thing," Cristiano says with laughter in his voice. "Your eyes were all wide but you were frowning. Very cute."

"Thanks?"

"You are welcome," Cristiano says, apparently not hearing the question in the statement. "Now remember to enjoy yourself! Get drunk, be happy. This is a new season! Come on!"

Cristiano drags him to the food table. Ruad has outdone himself. There are hors d'oeuvres: little pastries, wings, small sandwiches and cheese samples. Devon eats right off the platter like everyone else and sips at his cider. He doesn't want to get *too* drunk. He's got a job to do and Eldan to look forward to later. But a little buzz won't kill anyone.

He drifts, listening in on conversation after conversation, floating around the edges, and he smiles; this is where he belongs. Even if he's not in the middle of the action, maybe he's always been an "edges" kind of person. Maybe that's not such a bad thing. He can be the center of himself, and he already has people surrounding his edges: Eldan, Cristiano, Kelsi, Brandon,

Ruad—and he doesn't feel scattered. He's contained, as if he's really inhabiting his body. The thought grounds him, even as heady a feeling as it is.

"You look happy," Kelsi says, finding him near one of the fires just after the sun sets. "Eldan?"

Devon considers and glances over at Eldan, who is chatting animatedly with someone covered in tattoos, someone Devon doesn't know, and then shakes his head. "He's part of it, but no. Mostly I think it's me."

"Oooh, that's promising," Kelsi says. "You know you're home, right?"

"Yeah." It's not perfect, but it is what it is. He made his choice, and he's here now, entirely.

"Good," Kelsi says, hugging him. "You're good to have around, Devon. For all of us."

"Even for Maia?"

"Oh, who knows? For me, anyway. And definitely for Eldan." She grins at him, a little slyly. "You know, we have that to thank you for. He's been lonely a long time."

"Me too."

"Yeah. You too. But just remember, Eldan's a lot older than you think."

With that, she wanders off, leaving Devon to smile at the flames. Eldan may have been lonely for a lot longer than Devon has, but neither of them is lonely now. That's what matters, right?

Eventually, though, Eldan stands between the fires and holds up his hands. People spot him one by one and fall silent.

"Fellow Fae," Eldan calls out. "Brethren, sistren, siblingtren." Laughter and groans at the silliness. "Whatever you may be. Happy Beltane!"

Cheers erupt, and Eldan is clearly in his element, with a glow on his fair cheeks. Devon's never seen anyone so beautiful.

"Now. We all know why we're here: to be cleansed and to greet a new season of growth and fertility with open arms and open hearts. And I'm sure some other areas will open as well."

Cheers again, and a few leering jeers. Eldan grins.

"Now comes the time when we cleanse, though. When we burn away the old, the lingering, and bring luck to ourselves. If everyone would line up, please. And one by one, pass through the flames."

They gather in a ramshackle line around the far side of the bonfires, and then, one by one, walk steadily between the bonfires. On the cleansed side, the gathering starts cheering the others on, opening their arms and patting the newest person on the back, and then the next and the next and the next. It's clear to Devon then just how much a community they are, no matter how often they see each other.

Devon walks through, and surreality comes over him. Maybe the magic is working. Even though he's sweating, he feels cleaner, as if something in his heart gives way. The flames blast heat at him from either side as if they're actually burning away old trauma and loneliness and pain.

When he reaches the other side, he grins, and everyone greets him as enthusiastically as they greeted everyone else. And then, it's only fitting that he do the same. With each new addition to the group, he reaches out and touches, cheering and congratulating with the rest.

Finally, last of all, Eldan stands alone on the far side of the fire. He smiles softly, as if he knows something, and then stares at Devon as he walks gracefully with both hands out to the sides as though to feel the heat more strongly. As he gets close, his smile turns into a grin, and he finally laughs as everyone swarms around him, cheering louder than ever before as they welcome him.

But Eldan only has eyes for Devon. He follows him as he's shunted around, finally slipping through the group to grab Devon into a kiss.

Devon's ears ring with the cheers at that, and he pulls away, bashful under so much attention. But Eldan just grabs his hands and holds them.

"Don't be shy," Eldan says. "Most of these people will be openly fucking before the night is over."

Devon shakes his head. "I want you alone."

"Do a quick check with me, and we'll go," Eldan says. "Start the real party off right by disappearing."

Devon smiles and casts his mind out.

Someone is missing.

"Eldan," he says, a core of cold panic settling in his stomach. "Brandon's not here."

Eldan grips his arm and nods. "Can you cast your mind wider? Try to find him? Go through Céilí room by room if you have to."

Devon closes his eyes and tries to visualize each room in Céilí, starting with the fourth floor and working his way down. Nothing happens as he does a cursory brush of the fourth floor, but he hits something—something strange—a mind, yes, but it's almost impenetrable, and it *buzzes* inside Devon's skull.

"Third floor," Devon says. "It doesn't feel like Brandon though."

"Kelsi!" Eldan shouts. Devon jumps, startled, losing his touch with the strange buzzing mind.

Kelsi pushes through the crowd. "Yeah?"

"We've found a spy in our midst," Eldan says. "I need your strength with me."

Kelsi's brow furrows, but she just nods. "Lead the way."

ELDAN OPENS THE DOOR TO his room, and almost walks right into Brandon.

"Hey, guys," he says lightly. "Uh, Eldan, I was just gonna—"

"Kelsi," Eldan says, nodding her forward. "Him."

Kelsi grabs Brandon's arm. He cries out in dismay and pain.

"Hey, what the hell, guys?"

"Quit the act," Eldan says. "Devon, what does he feel like now?"

Devon reaches out and finds Brandon's mind still impenetrable, but no longer buzzing. "It's him. I'm hitting a wall. But it's not strange anymore."

"You were using the Queens' magic," Eldan says. "You are a Knight."

Brandon seems appropriately confused and horrified. "What's going on?" he asks. "Knight?"

"Well, then, let me in your head," Eldan says. "I'll have a good look around and you'll be absolved."

Brandon's eyes dart around, and then he bolts for the door. However, he's pulled up short by Kelsi, who tightens her grip and *hauls* Brandon back.

"Nope," she says, steadying him while maintaining her hold on him. "Not a chance."

Brandon mutters something, and Kelsi yelps. Her free hand grabs at the one holding Brandon, but she doesn't release him.

"Eldan, help!" she shrieks.

Eldan puts his hand on Brandon's head and *squeezes*, and Brandon gasps and sags.

"If you try anything more I will personally ensure your entire body's combustion," Eldan says in a frighteningly calm voice. "Now. Are you going to cooperate?"

Brandon gets his feet under himself and stands as Eldan releases his head slowly. Kelsi holds hard, switching hands and shaking out the one that was hurt.

"So you posed as a changeling and put yourself in our midst," Eldan says, frowning. "Who told you to do it?"

"Who do you think?" Brandon says. His voice is different; the tone of it is sharper, darker. His face doesn't match his bright blue hair; there's nothing joyous in it.

"And you pulled it off. Congratulations."

Brandon shrugs.

"Why?" Eldan asks. "Did we not provide you a home? A life?"

"What choice do I have? I'm in their thrall. They're the ones who give me my power and my life. I'm entirely in their hands."

"And did you want to?" Eldan crosses his arms.

Brandon peers up at him. "Why does it matter?"

"Because our next course of action relies heavily upon it. Now tell the truth. Did you want to spy on us?"

"No," Brandon says. He tilts his face down, and then back up again, keeping his mouth tight. "You guys are the only family I have."

Eldan nods. "I welcomed you as family, it's true. I thought you were one of us."

"But I'm human," Brandon says with the hint of a sneer. "Just because I wasn't born with powers I'm not *good enough* for you."

"Not quite," Eldan says. "If there's anything that makes you undesirable, it's your deceit, not your blood." He takes a breath as Brandon's face tightens.

"And what would you have had me do? I don't control my own life. I have to do what they say."

Eldan pauses, then says, "And how do they hold that over you while you're here? Their power doesn't extend to the human world."

Brandon grimaces and shakes his head. "You don't know. You don't know what they do. You don't know what they've done."

Eldan stares hard at him and then shakes his head slightly. He turns to Devon.

"A word?" he says. "Kelsi, you got him?"

Kelsi nods. "Yeah."

Eldan eyes Brandon. "Don't try anything, or it will go badly for you."

"It's going to go badly either way," Brandon says. "You've been gone too long. You don't remember their power. They hold everything in their sway."

Eldan shakes his head. "Not everything. Devon?"

Eldan leads Devon outside the bedroom, stopping just in the hallway, closing the door.

"I need to talk this out," Eldan says. "Listen?"

"Of course," Devon says.

"I think we have an opportunity here," Eldan says. "No matter what Brandon says, the Queens' power doesn't reach the human world. Not unless it's through Brandon himself. I don't think they have direct control over him from where they are."

"So?" Devon asks. "He's still in their thrall, he said so."

"I think he doesn't have to be. I think we could use him."

"How?"

"Let him do his job," Eldan says. "Let him tell the Queens what we're up to."

"I don't get it. Why?"

"Because we can keep apprised of what the Queens know. All Brandon has to do is keep doing what he's doing, but I'll watch him in return."

"Won't the Queens notice if you're lurking around during their calls, or whatever?"

"No, that's the thing. It's simply a reflection of what's happening on the other end of the line. They can't reach their magic through it; they don't have any actual power over here without the Knight—and we have their Knight now. They can't reach through it; they can only see through it. As long as I stay out of sight and keep my shields up, they won't know I'm there."

"But Brandon has to cooperate," Devon says. "What if he gives you away?"

"That's the risk we have to take. I believe him when he says we're his family; you can't fake that for this many years without slipping up. It's real."

"I don't know," Devon says. "I think it's perfectly possible that he is faking it and just saying that to save his own skin."

Eldan sighs. "I'll have to get into his head. I don't know if we're compatible, or if that even matters with humans. It's going to be complicated. But I have to try."

"I could do it," Devon says. "If you teach me how."

Eldan considers. "You know, that might be an idea. Cristiano could do it, too. Maybe—hmm."

"What?"

"Maybe all three of us will have to do it." Eldan rubs his face. "This is something we simply don't need right now. Gods."

Devon reaches out and puts his hands on Eldan's shoulders, squeezing and rubbing. "You can do this. *We* can do this."

Eldan rests his hands on top of Devon's and presses his forehead against Devon's. "Thank you for saying that."

"We should get back in there," Devon says. "I feel nervous about leaving Kelsi alone with him."

"You're right," Eldan says. "We'll put this to him. And see what happens. Okay?"

"If you think that's best," Devon says. "Let's do it."

ELDAN STANDS BEFORE BRANDON AGAIN, who is passive in Kelsi's grip.

"You're a traitor," Eldan says. "You took our trust and you twisted it to your own ends. You lied to us, you spied on us, you betrayed us."

Brandon says nothing. He just stares at Eldan, face neutral.

"But."

Devon glances carefully over at Eldan's face. It's relaxed but for the eyes, which flare dangerously.

"But?" Devon asks, hearing the word tumble from his mouth before he can stop it.

Eldan raises an eyebrow, as though rebuking him for ruining the tension, before turning back to Brandon. "But."

Brandon breathes heavily, a grimace on his face. "But what?"

"But maybe, just maybe, I have a way for you to redeem yourself."

Brandon's eyes go wide. "You'd give me a second chance?"

"Oh, with conditions," Eldan says fiercely. "First one being you let me into your head so I know the truth."

Brandon's grimace deepens, but he nods. "Okay. I'll think about that—"

"That's not all. You will report to me before you report to your Queens. I will approve what you say, and any suggestions I make for improvement will be taken. And they will know nothing of this arrangement."

"You want me to deceive the Queens?" Brandon asks. "Do you know how dangerous that is? They don't need my permission to see into my head, Eldan; they have total control over me."

"And what will they do to you if you are caught?" Eldan asks mildly, as though the conversation is light and unconcerning.

Brandon's face pales and he swallows. "Not—not good things."

Eldan nods. "So. Which is your better option?"

"If they catch on—"

"I have certain tricks I can teach you, to better your chances," Eldan says. "And I'll be right there every time you talk to them. If you agree, that is. I have further conditions."

"What are they?"

"You will be monitored at all times. All of our core family will be alerted to your true nature and told all of what's been said here, and you will have to earn back our trust. Am I clear?"

He nods, sharp and quick.

"Good." Eldan smiles. "Then do we have a deal?"

Brandon sighs, and then holds out his right hand. Eldan takes it, shaking it once before pulling Brandon in.

"And if you harm any one of my family or friends," he says, hissing low and dangerous, "I will make the Queens look like the better option. Is that understood?"

Brandon winces, as though Eldan is hurting him, and then he nods. "Yes. I'll keep my powers to myself."

"Good." Eldan releases him. "Then we're done."

"You know we won't get away with this forever," Brandon says. "I'm sentencing myself either way."

"Then we will have to come up with a plan to protect you," Eldan says. "Now. You're going to your rooms, and I will lock you in for the night. And trust me, you won't get past my spells. Then, tomorrow morning, the others will be told. And your sentence will begin."

Brandon just nods. He appears vaguely ill, but Devon doesn't have much of a chance to study him, because Kelsi marches him out. Eldan gives Devon a smile.

"Wait for me?"

Devon nods. "I'll be here."

WHEN ELDAN RETURNS, HE SIGHS, looking tired. "It's done."

Devon takes Eldan's hands. "What do you need right now?" he asks, knowing that this is affecting Eldan more than he's letting on. One of his own has betrayed him—Devon can't even imagine how deeply that must hurt.

"I need you," Eldan says. "Please."

Devon kisses him, and Eldan melts into his body. Devon lets him, content to be leaned on as he's needed.

"Take me to my room?" Eldan requests softly.

"Anything," Devon says.

Eldan takes his hand and leads him into his rooms.

Eldan's room has a dimmer. When they walk in, Eldan switches it to a low, romantic lighting, and Devon is unable to keep from laughing. Eldan shrugs, smiling, simply saying, "I get headaches."

Devon moves automatically. He shucks off his shirt and pants; Eldan does the same. Then, with most of their clothes removed, they crawl into bed, and Devon is happy to appreciate Eldan in the low light. His body is long and lithe and the dips and contours are mesmerizing as Devon explores them with his fingertips, slowly, carefully.

"You feel very good," Eldan says, gripping Devon's biceps. "Please don't stop."

"I won't," Devon promises, feeling remarkably at ease. He's in control, as if he has a handle on things, and they're finally happening the way he wants them to. It's satisfying, and Eldan doesn't seem to mind handing over the reins to Devon.

"Good," Eldan says, sinking back onto the bed. Devon rolls over until he's half-sitting up with one arm free to brush lightly down beneath Eldan's belly button.

Eldan writhes as Devon skims down to the edge of his briefs.

"Do you want me to take them off?" Devon asks calmly.

Eldan lifts his hips and nods. "Please."

Devon peels them down slowly, eyes riveted on what's revealed. Eldan's cock is just as beautiful as the rest of him, rosy red and long. But Devon doesn't stare long, just until he has to look down to get the briefs off Eldan's long legs.

"You're beautiful," he says, leaning over Eldan and kissing him.

Eldan grasps at his back, pulling him down farther, dipping one hand to push impatiently at Devon's own underwear. He gets it halfway off Devon's ass before Devon pulls back, laughing, and shucks them down himself.

"Come back," Eldan requests, and Devon is only too happy to press himself along Eldan's body. Eldan opens up for him, spreads his legs and pulls Devon between them. Devon settles into him, lining up and rocking their groins together with a casual thrust.

"No, come *here*," Eldan says, and Devon goes down to kiss him.

"Do you want to fuck me?" Eldan asks between kisses. "Mmm?"

"Yeah," Devon says. "Where's—"

"Bedside table, where else?"

Devon pulls out lube and rips a condom from a long strip of them. Then, he returns to Eldan.

"God," he says, looking down at Eldan, open and waiting for him. He's *stunning*. "God, I just—Eldan—"

"I know," Eldan says, cupping his face. "I feel it, too."

Devon kisses him, then shifts to kneel between Eldan's legs. And then, pops the cap off the lube and drizzles it on his fingers.

"Here," Devon says. "Let me stretch you."

He reaches down and strokes with one slick finger in the crease between Eldan's cheeks. He's warm and wrinkled and easy, and opens for the first finger readily. Devon takes a moment to mouth at Eldan's chest and just *feel* him once the finger is all the way in; he's so warm and tight. But two fingers ease in fine, and then three.

"You ready?" Devon asks, spearing him open steadily. Eldan wriggles impatiently.

"Undoubtedly," he says.

Devon laughs, withdraws his fingers and wipes them on his own thigh before retrieving the condom and slipping it on. He grabs the lube bottle and applies a generous amount before he returns his attention all the way to Eldan.

"You're incredible," he says, as Eldan's thighs part farther and his hands wander over Devon's shoulders.

"Then let me prove it," Eldan chuckles. "Get in me already."

Devon laughs again, but he grows serious as he lines up and pushes in.

"That's right," Eldan says, closing his eyes and rocking his hips against Devon, taking him in deeper. "Just like that."

Devon leans forward onto his hands, hovering above Eldan as he slides fully inside. "Like that?"

Eldan smiles wickedly. "I'm not sure. Do it again."

Devon grins and complies.

AFTER, THEY LIE SIDE BY side, hands held between them, heads turned to face each other, breathing each other's air.

"Stay?" Eldan asks.

Devon nods. "You're not getting rid of me."

"Never. My mate."

"Yes," Devon says. If it makes Eldan happy, he can indulge this. Maybe even try to believe it. "I am."

EPILOGUE

THREE MONTHS LATER DEVON AND Eldan have a big day ahead of them.

Devon's nervous about this. It's fast, it's so fast, but over these past three months Eldan has proven time and again that they're meant for each other, and Devon has started to believe about being mates. After all, he believes in everything else—why not open his heart to this? Today is the day the mating ceremony is supposed to happen: August 1st. *Lugnasad*, Eldan said, spelling it out on a napkin.

This day is about choice. He's not *destined*, but rather suited, to be with Eldan. He has to make the decision to commit to that himself. And Eldan wants it, he wants it before Céilí opens and whirls their life into something new. He wants something to hold onto, Devon suspects. And Devon, despite his nerves, is happy to give him that, because he might need something to hold onto as well.

After breakfast, Eldan finds him and, smiling and wordless, he reaches out to Devon. Together they weave through the bar and kitchen and storeroom and head out back, where Ruad's truck is waiting for them.

Devon hops in the passenger seat, and Eldan drives. Together, they head out of the city and into the hills. They hold hands, and Devon enjoys the summer air rushing past his open window.

Eldan smiles. "So. This ceremony today. It's for a year and a day, okay?"

"What's for a year and a day? The ceremony?" Devon is terribly confused.

"No, the commitment. We're not getting married. We commit to each other for a year and a day. And next year, if we want to, we can do a permanent ceremony."

"Like marriage."

Eldan blushes heavily. "Yes, basically."

"So what we're doing today is getting engaged?" Devon asks, mostly to tease Eldan. He enjoys riling up Eldan, who is awkward about this.

"It's—no. There's no obligation to marry. If we want to part ways in a year, we can. No commitment beyond this year."

"But there's an understanding that it's headed *toward* marriage, yeah?"

"We can always recommit for another year if we want. No need to do the permanent ceremony if we're not ready."

Devon squeezes Eldan's hand. "I'm pulling your leg, Eldan. We'll see where we are when it comes."

Eldan sighs, relaxing. "I was hoping you'd see it that way."

Devon shrugs; the nerves started to abate when he was teasing Eldan, and the drive is beautiful as they leave the city and get up into the hills.

"What are the others gonna do today?" Devon's been keeping out of the planning phase of this. Eldan asked to handle it.

"They're headed up to Griffith to play some games and have a picnic and get drunk," Eldan says. Devon knows that includes Brandon, who's been cooperative so far. "We'll skip those festivities. But Serena should be waiting for us up here."

They reach a parking area. From there, it's a hike, holding hands between them as they wind their way up, up, up the path.

At the top is a gorgeous view, and Serena is waiting with a basket beside her. There's a bottle in it, and two glasses and a ribbon.

"Hey, guys," she says with a wide smile. "You ready for this?"

Eldan and Devon pause to catch their breath, nodding and grinning.

"Great!" she says. "Come on, no one cares if you're out of shape, just get over here and get together."

They stand in front of her, holding hands with Eldan's left hand in Devon's right. Serena takes the ribbon from her basket, and then lifts their joined hands and holds them in her tiny hands, with the ribbon dangling.

"Do you both commit to one another for the next year and a day?"

Devon notices the magic; it tingles in his fingertips as Serena winds the ribbon over and under and around their wrists and hands.

"Yes," Devon says. Eldan echoes him. His hair is blowing in the breeze, and he is smiling gently. Devon can't take his eyes off him.

"Then be together, and keep this knot tied until the next ceremony of *Lugnasad*. On that day, if you wish to move further, present the tied knot to me and exchange rings. If you'd rather recommit, a new ribbon will be tied. If you do not, untie the knot and bring me the severed ends of this ribbon, and move forward apart."

She ties the knot and pulls it tight. Then, she pulls a knife from her belt and makes a precise cut. The ribbon ends fall, and Eldan unwinds it from their wrists, leaving them with two loose ends and a knot in the center.

"I'm done here," Serena says. "You boys have a good night."

She heads to the path, leaving Eldan and Devon alone with the bottle and the glasses.

"What's that?" Devon asks.

Eldan tucks the ribbon carefully into the basket, and pulls out the bottle and the glasses.

"Bilberry wine!" Eldan says. "You have to have bilberries today. It's tradition. But no one said *how* you have to have them, so we made them into a drink."

Devon laughs. "Fine. Let's drink up."

Eldan pours the wine. He holds his glass out. "To us."

Devon grins. "To us."

THEY ONLY HAVE ONE GLASS before they head down the hill and back home. They don't want to be drunk when they go to Eldan's room, which is more and more *their* room, and they're happy to have clear heads as they undress and fall into bed.

"Are you ready?" Devon asks quietly, holding Eldan's hand.

"I love you," Eldan whispers, when Devon is fully sheathed inside of him. He hitches his legs up around Devon's waist, holds Devon's face between his hands, and breathes it. "I love you so much."

"I love you too," Devon says, smiling down at Eldan. His forehead is beaded with sweat, his eyes are shining, he's trembling and Devon is, too.

They've bonded in the old way, handfasted and promised themselves to each other, and it's as though every piece of their hearts has bloomed, spread, made more room to hold the love for each other that has been steadily growing in the three months since they settled into each other.

And now here they are. Bonded soul mates. Promised to each other, to one day be linked inexorably. They will live every day together. And they will, one day, die together, and travel to the next life with their connection only strengthened, ready to find each other again. At least, that's what Eldan believes. Devon's working on it.

But now, Devon's completely cloaked in the feeling of their bond, and he closes his eyes, overwhelmed by it. Even completely enveloped by Eldan, he doesn't feel grounded. So he turns his head, kisses Eldan's wrist, around which the ribbon was wound. He barely brushes it, but Eldan clenches around him and then lets out a weak cry, arching beneath him. He pulls back and kisses Eldan's parted lips and begins to rock inside him.

"God, Eldan, you feel so good," Devon whimpers, nuzzling Eldan's cheek and trying to keep a slow, steady pace, tempted by the feeling of Eldan tight around his cock to just let go and fuck him until they're both coming. But not tonight.

"You do too," Eldan gasps in return, twisting his hips up to match Devon's thrusts, pulling him in harder, deeper. "Oh fuck—Devon, please—please, stay here with me—"

"I'm not going anywhere," Devon promises, holding Eldan tight. He knows exactly how Eldan feels—as if even this close isn't close enough, as if they can't ever have too much of each other, as if they'll shatter and break if they ever have to part. It's an irrational worry, but Devon wants to be surrounded by Eldan completely, to feel him on every nerve in his body. He settles for kissing his mate and fucking him just a little harder. "I'm not going anywhere, Eldan. I'm right here with you."

Eldan sobs and abandons himself to Devon. The trust is heady, and Devon is determined to always make that trust worth it for Eldan, to keep it safe and make this the most satisfying experience possible for both of them.

"Let me in?" Devon requests quietly, threading their fingers together.

Eldan nods, eyes half-shut, fingers scrabbling at Devon's back, holding him close. Devon smiles and leans down, adjusting enough to give Eldan the best angle. He leans their foreheads together.

And then he drops every barrier, and they let each other in.

They don't do it often. It's intense, and it has collateral effects. But everyone knows what tonight is, and they're still out in the hills celebrating the holiday and leaving the two lovers to their peace. This night is for them alone, and they don't have to care if they lose control. It's just them in the world, now.

It's finally as though an itch has been scratched for Devon, being that close to Eldan, letting Eldan see into his heart like this, and Eldan letting him in as well, returning the trust. It's as if Devon sees all of him, as if they're inside each other's skin, as if they're surrounded by each other. And there's a feedback loop. Devon, after all, has a special talent for pushing his emotions and thoughts into others, and while he's developed other powers that supplement that, it's still the base of his power. He gives Eldan every throb of pleasure, every sweet, stinging beat of his heart, every spark down his spine when Eldan squeezes him tight. And in return, he takes what Eldan feels—all the aching fullness, the sharp spikes of his own pleasure, and the trembling vulnerability of being so taken apart—and feeds it back to Eldan, back and forth and back and forth until he's pounding into Eldan, crying out and wrapping him up and tugging him down as he thrusts up, jolting desperate wails from Eldan's mouth.

"Oh, fuck, I love you," Devon groans, and Eldan whimpers incoherently and holds Devon close with arms and legs and the hot clasp of his ass, over and over and over. "Fuck, Eldan—I'm gonna—fuck—"

"Devon—"

The sharp build of pleasure crests, and Devon comes, mouth open, silent, body seized tight, matching Eldan's below him as Eldan spills hard over their stomachs, exhaling broken, sobbing cries where he's pressed his face against Devon's shoulder, too open, too revealed to let himself be exposed to anything but Devon.

They lie in silence and in darkness for a long time, holding on to the feeling that they are truly, entirely together. But finally, Devon's dick slips free of Eldan's body, accompanied by a little grunt from Devon.

Eldan snickers and whispers, "Are you alive?"

Devon wants to give him a witty reply, but he just grunts, and Eldan laughs again, shaking under Devon.

"You're heavy, get off," he says. Devon smacks his thigh lightly and then rolls to the side, pulling him along. "Can you talk?"

"Yes," Devon replies sleepily. "But why?"

"Because I want you to tell me you love me," Eldan says. Devon smiles. "I love you."

"I love you, too."

Céilí OPENS THREE MONTHS LATER.

They've had soft openings, of course. Parties, gatherings, each one carefully catered to whomever the guest was. Eldan marketed them to the right people, calling in favors that belonged to all the Fae who ever attended Céilí, working his way up the social ladder until he got party reservations from celebrities.

And he hosted special events, leaving Céilí closed between events to build the gossip, the curiosity. But now it's time to open to the public. There's plenty of buzz, and Eldan is ready, Devon knows. They're all ready.

Eldan sits with Devon at a table for two, where his throne used to be. The curtain has been taken down. Eldan uses his own rooms as an office now. And it's not the only thing that's changed: The tables are now smaller, square so they match up if needed, with only four chairs at each, and the bar is restocked with new drinks named more accessibly. Ruad has a stable menu, and the acts have a new rota. The fourth floor is completely cleaned and a few rooms are occupied, but most of the floor has private rooms for any guests who might need them. Maia has used them many times.

And the glamour is down. Céilí is officially on the map, no longer hidden to passersby. Tonight, there's a line down the street of people waiting to get in. Kelsi is at the door waiting for Eldan's signal.

Eldan sits at his table with Devon, fidgeting with the walkie-talkie that connects to five others: two at the bar, one in the kitchen, one backstage and one with Kelsi. Devon waits patiently. Eldan will talk when he's ready.

"This is it," he finally says, smiling over at Devon. "What we've been waiting for. Sink or swim."

Devon smiles back, nodding. "Mmhm."

"Don't 'mmhm' me," Eldan says. "I am having a moment."

"Sorry. Go ahead."

"Thank you," Eldan says and then grows more serious. "Really. Thank you. Without you, I don't know if I would've had the courage to do this."

Devon takes Eldan's hand and squeezes. "Sure you would've. You'd do anything for this place."

Eldan casts around, eyes shining. "I would."

"Okay," Devon says. "So do it."

Eldan grins. "Fine, I will."

He holds up the walkie-talkie and presses the button.

"Kelsi, we are ready to go," Eldan says. "Let them in."

Devon kisses Eldan, just once. "For luck."

Eldan's grin widens. "We don't need it, baby."

Behind them, the doors open.

ACKNOWLEDGMENTS

FIRST, I'D LIKE TO THANK the team at Interlude for their continued amazing work—especially Annie, Candy and Choi, and all the love in the world to Lex, who left us too soon. I wouldn't be where I am without the support of all the Interlude team.

Big thanks to Jude, for being my sounding board, my unofficial editor, my second pair of eyes and, most of all, my best friend. This book has pieces of you in it, and I am so grateful for that, because it makes it more beautiful.

More thanks to Ali, who got me writing again after a long dry spell. You started my fandom journey by encouraging me to post my first fic, and it was the beginning of so many words from me. You woke me up and gave me something to strive for when my life had so little purpose. Thank you, from the bottom of my heart, you darling angel.

Further thanks to Meg, for the insight into California, and for always being a fan of my work, and to Noemie for the early help. And thank you to Danee, for the hard advice, and to Caroline, for the time you gave me.

Thanks to my family—my husband and my son, mostly for going to sleep early and leaving me alone at night so I could actually write this thing. And for listening when I needed to complain or ache or untangle things in my head.

And a big thank you to the continued support and love from my community, my friends, on Tumblr. I would be nowhere without your encouragement and curiosity and all the things you had to teach me.

ABOUT THE AUTHOR

MORIAH GEMEL STARTED WRITING AT the tender age of seven, after her grandfather gave her her first novel. Ever since, she has been a fan of fantasy novels and decided it was high time to write one herself. Passionate about diversity in fiction, Moriah is dedicated to writing realistic romances for many audiences. Her first novel, *Load the Dice*, was first published as a ten-part serial. Moriah lives in Central New York with her husband, young son, and two cats.

interludepress™

interludepress.com
@InterludePress
interludepress
store.interludepress.com

interlude  press

now available...

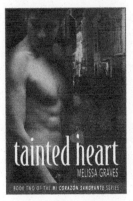